"I have no second thoughts," Tariq reiterated with the will of iron for which he was renowned. **"The wedding makes sense. It has to happen."**

"Yes. And it doesn't hurt that your intended bride is utterly stunning, I suppose."

Tariq considered that, trying to conjure a mental image of the crown princess. Only there was another pair of eyes that flooded his brain, wide-set and the creamiest almond butter–brown with flecks of gold and thick dark lashes. A heart-shaped face with a dainty ski-jump nose and a swanlike neck that was perfectly in proportion to her fine-boned, dainty body.

Eloise.

Even just her name had an effect on him, so he ground his teeth together, forcing his legendary focus onto the matter at hand.

He hadn't been with a woman since his father fell ill. His body was craving what he could not have— and it was abundantly clear that the very best friend of his future wife was not a suitable partner. Any and all fantasies from this point on were strictly forbidden.

The Long-Lost Cortéz Brothers

Two powerful men...and the shocking secret that binds them!

In the aftermath of the tragic accident that killed their family, Graciano Cortéz was ripped apart from the younger brother he'd vowed to protect. Graciano has never stopped looking for him, even while he was building his billion-dollar empire from the ground up.

Then, his decades-long search leads him to the palace doors of Sheikh Tariq al Hassan of Savisia... Will he finally be reunited with his long-lost sibling? And will the road to their reunion bring both Graciano and Tariq more than they bargained for—life-changing desire?

After ten years apart, a shocking reunion will force Graciano to face the woman he never forgot and the secret she keeps that will rock his world...

Read Graciano and Alicia's story in
The Secret She Must Tell the Spaniard

Royal advisor Eloise is tasked with approving her queen's suitor, Sheikh Tariq, which is complicated by the undeniable chemistry erupting between *her* and Tariq!

Read Tariq and Eloise's story in
Desert King's Forbidden Temptation

Both available now!

Clare Connelly

DESERT KING'S FORBIDDEN TEMPTATION

HARLEQUIN®

PRESENTS™

Recycling programs for this product may not exist in your area.

ISBN-13: 978-1-335-58447-2

Desert King's Forbidden Temptation

Copyright © 2023 by Clare Connelly

For questions and comments about the quality of this book, please contact us at CustomerService@Harlequin.com.

Harlequin Enterprises ULC
22 Adelaide St. West, 41st Floor
Toronto, Ontario M5H 4E3, Canada
www.Harlequin.com

Printed in U.S.A.

Clare Connelly was raised in small-town Australia among a family of avid readers. She spent much of her childhood up a tree, Harlequin book in hand. Clare is married to her own real-life hero, and they live in a bungalow near the sea with their two children. She is frequently found staring into space—a surefire sign she is in the world of her characters. She has a penchant for French food and ice-cold champagne, and Harlequin novels continue to be her favorite-ever books. Writing for Harlequin Presents is a long-held dream. Clare can be contacted via clareconnelly.com or on her Facebook page.

Books by Clare Connelly

Harlequin Presents

Crowned for His Desert Twins
Emergency Marriage to the Greek
Pregnant Princess in Manhattan

Passionately Ever After...

Cinderella in the Billionaire's Castle

The Cinderella Sisters

Vows on the Virgin's Terms
Forbidden Nights in Barcelona

The Long-Lost Cortéz Brothers

The Secret She Must Tell the Spaniard

Visit the Author Profile page
at Harlequin.com for more titles.

PROLOGUE

THE WATER WAS always darkest near the surface, though that wasn't how it was meant to be. There, in the inches beneath atmosphere and air, there was supposed to be light, the sun's warmth permeating the thickness of the sea. Always, the water at the top shimmered. But this wasn't reality, it was a dream, a nightmare, and the laws of physics need not be obeyed.

He sucked inwards, seeking air, finding only water, drowning, reaching out, touching, feeling, remembering. Something foreign yet achingly familiar, close but always, always out of reach. The nearer he came to remembering, to catching the threads that danced on the periphery of his unconscious, the more they shimmied beyond his reach. A fleeting touch, soft and infinitely comforting, a fragrance—vanilla and persimmon—sunlight dancing on ancient timber floor boards, dust motes and laughter—his, and someone else's, a voice, a faraway, long-ago voice without a face.

Frustration gnawed and burst him from his dream; a young boy had been drowning, unable to find purchase in the darkness of the ocean's depths, but now a sheikh awoke, showing not a hint of the nightmare that had taunted him.

There were mysteries in his past, questions that dogged him when he allowed them to slip beyond his defences, but of one thing he was certain: the duty to rule Savisia was his and his alone, and Sheikh Tariq al Hassan would fulfil that destiny with his dying breath. Whatever was required of him, he would offer gladly. He owed this country that much, at least.

CHAPTER ONE

IT WASN'T SOMETHING she'd consciously sought, but nonetheless, it was an undeniable fact that Eloise Ashworth had become masterful at studying and understanding people. Like all skills, it had been borne of necessity, and her tumultuous young life, with parents who fought viciously nonstop, then her existence after their deaths, had sharpened already keen powers of observation.

Now, they were impossible to switch off, so she found her eyes lingering on the Sheikh's face for a moment too long. Where others might have simply glimpsed a look of benign disinterest, Eloise saw beyond it, to the small furrow of his brow, the slight narrowing of his eyes, the very barely noticeable clenching of his jaw, and she wondered—how could she not?—what had happened to frustrate him?

The obvious answer was that he wanted to avoid this marriage. That he didn't welcome it. Given that his palace had proposed it, three months earlier, that didn't make much sense. Unless someone else was pulling the strings? Her eyes swept the six men who flanked the powerful Sheikh of Savisia; she discounted the idea almost immediately. For no reason she could put her finger on, she didn't for a moment believe the powerful Sheikh was someone who could be made to do a thing he didn't want to. The marriage had been his idea, only he didn't like it, she was sure of it.

She leaned back a little farther in her seat, studying him quite openly. After all, no one was looking at her. Of the twelve people gathered to discuss the possibility of this match, she was the only woman, and the only attendee who didn't hold government office. She suspected her opinion and insights weren't of much value—even her seat was at the far end of the table, and not once had a single head turned in her direction, to ask for her thoughts. Ironic, really, given her best friend in the whole world, Crown Princess Elana of Ras Sarat, had sent Eloise with the sole purpose of determining if the marriage should go ahead. After all, the Sheikh had somewhat of a glittering reputation: he was heroic, intelligent, staunchly patriotic and adored by his people, but that didn't give any insight into what he was like as a man. In fact, his private life was incredibly well guarded, so repeated internet searches had brought up a heap of photographs at official events but nothing of interest beyond that.

And so, Eloise had been sent to evaluate the man, the potential of the marriage, and to go back to Ras Sarat ready to advise Elana.

It was Eloise alone that Elana would listen to; her counsel the only voice that would matter in determining if Elana would consent to the match. Oh, she wanted to marry Sheikh Tariq—or rather, Elana accepted the necessity of it. The truth, however, was that she didn't want to marry anyone, and if she'd been a private citizen, she would have grieved for her late fiancé for the rest of her life. Elana had loved deeply, and lost, and she wasn't likely to ever love again. But that wasn't what this prospective union was about: theirs would be a marriage of political expediency.

For all that Tariq's kingdom was large and fabulously wealthy, Ras Sarat was small, and decades of mismanagement had left it in a parlous financial and political state. Marriage to a man like Tariq would shore up her government and provide a badly needed influx of money. It would also take an enormous burden off Elana's shoulders—a burden no one but Eloise understood she carried—and for this reason, Eloise desperately wanted to like the Sheikh. To believe he would be a good husband for her friend, that the marriage would work.

And so she watched him: as he spoke, but also, as he listened, and it was in these moments that she saw the most. The small flex of his jaw when he disagreed with something someone was saying, the inclining of his chin as he considered a point, the tightening around his mouth and eyes. His face remained quite expressionless for the most part, but she read beyond that. She saw the minute body language shifts that caused the air around him to reverberate, silent signals that she alone seemed aware of.

Papers were shuffled, chairs scraped back, and Eloise sat perfectly still, though now, it had less to do with the Sheikh's responses and more to do with a strange heaviness in her legs that made it impossible to move. She was staring at him to learn what she could of the man but somehow, something had shifted, and now her eyes lingered not for this purpose but rather, out of a selfish desire to see and study. Out of a hunger to look at him.

She was familiar with his appearance thanks to her internet snooping and the security file she and Elana had pored over. But there was something about him that didn't translate to two dimensional images. Where he was clearly handsome, there was a magnetism and charisma in real life that was impossible to ignore.

He was…spellbinding, and in that moment, for the briefest second, she felt the spell weave around her, ensnaring her exactly where she was.

As if he sensed her momentary weakness, in the flurry of activity as other advisors and diplomats pushed away from the table to take a short recess, his eyes sought the calm of the room, and landed with a thud on her.

They were beautiful eyes. Fascinating and shifting, compelling and magnetic, so that she couldn't do the wise thing and look away. Instead, her gaze locked to his, sparking something unfamiliar and unwanted in her bloodstream, making her conscious of every breath she took, of the way the hairs on her arms lifted.

He studied her with the same level of scrutiny she'd been regarding him with for the past hour, only this was far more pointed, more obvious. More entitled. He was a sheikh, and even if his personal bearing left anyone in any doubt of that, which it didn't, the room in which they sat would have served to underscore his incredible wealth and power. Enormous, with ceilings at least three times the normal height and a full wall of windows that overlooked a spectacular garden with pools of water and ancient date palms forming a spiky barrier, the walls were gold, the table a solid marble, and the Sheikh sat at a large chair, only slightly less dramatic than a throne—at its centre, commanding easily. He'd been raised to rule, his duty from birth had been to claim his birthright. With the death of his father, the beloved Sheikh Samir al Hassan, five months earlier, Tariq had taken on the role he'd been groomed for all of his life.

He was adored by his people—he always had been, ever since his parents had assumed the throne and he'd been catapulted into the role of heir apparent.

After that, his birthright had become an imperative—he embodied all the traits his people most admired. He was brave, honourable, strong, fearless. Not only was he Sheikh—he became a teen idol, a heart throb, a celebrity feted and adored by all.

He regarded Eloise now with absolute impunity.

He studied without a hint of apology.

And when finally, Eloise gathered her wits sufficiently to push back her own chair, and reach for her folder with slightly trembling hands, he spoke in a voice that didn't invite a hint of dissent.

'You will remain a moment.'

She'd been listening to him speak all morning, so why did *these* words make her bones feel as though they were melting into puddles of nothing?

She lifted a hand and pressed it to her chest, between her breasts. 'Me?'

She cringed inwardly at the weakness the query showed, but his command had rattled her.

Until that second, she hadn't realised how much she was looking forward to leaving the room and drawing in a deep breath. To looking at something *other* than this man.

He dipped his head once then gestured to the chair opposite him. 'Please.'

It was not said in the way 'please' usually was. This was no plea, no query of hopefulness. There was no expectation of a refusal. Suddenly, she was conscious of everything: the swish of her long, linen skirt as she moved around the table; the knocking of her knees; the shimmer of light streaming through the window and bouncing off the mahogany tabletop; the size of the room and the echo of his voice; the time it took—seconds that felt like years—to reach the chair opposite him; the feeling of the timber beneath her fingertips, cool and smooth, worn and ancient; his eyes on her with the same unashamed curiosity she'd exhibited all morning. She drew back the chair and sat into it. As a child, Eloise had studied dance. In fact, she'd lived for it, and though her great aunt hadn't approved of the lessons, the innate sense of grace and musicality hadn't left Eloise; it was evident even in the small motion of sitting down.

Only once seated did she drag her eyes to his, and the moment they connected, her bloodstream seemed to come to life for the very first time.

She could *feel* it in her veins, rushing like a river, gushing through her, her arteries paper thin, almost unable to cope with the frantic deluge.

He was the Sheikh; this was his palace, his meeting, his request that she stay, and so Eloise sat perfectly still and silent even when her unending curiosity, combined with suddenly jangling nerves, had her wanting to blurt out the question: What do you want?

But she stayed as she was, hands clasped in her lap to disguise the telltale trembling, knees pressed hard together, body strangely energised and tingling all over.

'You were not introduced.'

Her lips pulled to the side in a wry acknowledgement of the fact. 'No, Your Highness, I wasn't.' What more could she say? That the Ras Sarat advisors didn't see the purpose for her being on this trip? That they'd fought her tooth and nail over every issue since her official appointment as one of Elana's advisors? If only they knew how vital her assessment would be in shaping this marriage. If Eloise reported back to Elana anything negative, then there would be no marriage, no union, and none of these negotiations would matter at all.

'Let's rectify that now.' Again, it was an order, rather than a suggestion, and this was no mere formality. There was a sharpness to his words, and she understood something else important about the man: he liked to be in possession of all the facts. He was wary and private. Negotiating this marriage was unpalatable to him, for some reason, but if he had to do it, it would be in front of trusted advisors only, not random women from foreign countries. 'Your name?'

'Eloise, Your Highness.' His eyes widened and then darkened, and her blood heated at the speculation she saw in his gaze. Her heartbeat kicked up a gear.

'Eloise?' he prompted, his voice rough and incredibly appealing. It was a shame that Elana had sworn she'd never like, much less love, her future husband. Eloise understood how badly heartbroken her friend was, but Sheikh Tariq would be quite easy to fancy.

Easy to fancy?

Easy to fantasise about, more like.

'Ashworth,' she added.

'English?'

She nodded.

'And yet you work for the royal family of Ras Sarat?'

'Yes, Your Highness.' 'Royal family' though, was a misnomer. There was only Elana and an old uncle related by marriage, who had ostensibly served as a regent for Elana in the years between her father's death and Elana's coming of age.

Again, his eyes flexed in that fascinating way, and something low in her abdomen stirred. She shifted a little in her seat, then wished she hadn't, because awareness was flooding her veins, and heating her most feminine parts, so she had to dig her fingernails into her palms to get a grip on the situation.

'For how long?'

She tilted her head to the side, torn between her duty as a representative of Ras Sarat and her confidence as a woman of the twenty-first century. The former won out—just. 'Three years.'

He frowned. 'You don't look old enough.'

Her smile was laced with a hint of amusement. 'I'm twenty-five, Your Highness.'

He rubbed a hand over his chin. 'The same age as the Princess.'

'Yes.'

'Do you know her well?'

'Yes.'

He leaned forward a little, eyes scanning her face. 'You're friends?'

Surprise at his perceptiveness held her silent a moment, but after a beat, she said, 'Yes.'

'Close friends?'

'You could say that.'

He lifted a brow and she had to remind herself that he was a powerful ruler of this wealthy country. For some reason, she found it easy to speak with him as an equal, but he wasn't, and their difference in rank needed to be observed.

'We're close, yes, Your Highness,' she murmured with deference.

His eyes narrowed once again. 'And she asked you to come to these negotiations and report back to her?'

Eloise hadn't expected the challenge, but it didn't bother her. She was used to being challenged, and if he wouldn't accept her presence, then the marriage would be in serious trouble. 'Is that a problem?'

'Not at all.' He surprised her by responding instantly. 'It's wise. The Princess and I met some years ago, but only briefly. I'd consider her a fool indeed to agree to this without a little more information.'

'Her advisors will assess the merits of the match,' she said after a moment, strangely pleased by his reasonable reply. 'But my job is… of a more personal nature.'

'I see.' And he *did* see, of that she was certain. If Eloise was an expert at reading people, then it was a skill she was certain she shared with this man. 'And if you don't approve?'

'The rest of the delegation is thrilled with your proposal,' she said instead.

'I am asking about your approval, though.'

She hedged the question again. 'Is there a reason you think I won't approve, Your Highness?'

His lips quirked in a quick sign of appreciation of her response. 'I don't know enough about you to say. After all, your own life experiences will colour your judgement, will they not?'

'I try to be impartial when advising Her Highness.'

'Even on matters such as this?'

She lifted her slender shoulders. 'This is the first marriage proposal I've considered on her behalf.'

Another quirk of his lips and her heart lifted. She liked seeing him smile. She really liked it. That scared her into straightening, the smile slipping from her face completely, her features assuming a mask of cool command.

'Does my presence bother you, Your Highness?'

'No.' His eyes homed in on hers. 'But your answers are illuminating.'

'Oh?' Her heart kicked up a gear.

'Am I right in presuming your input will matter most to the Princess?'

Her lips parted in surprise and his gaze dropped swiftly to her mouth, lingering for just long enough to scatter her thoughts in a billion directions, before his attention moved back to her eyes.

Eloise licked her lower lip, frowning a little.

'It is not a difficult question.'

'Isn't it?' she murmured, lips once more pulling to the side in an unconscious gesture of amusement.

'You tell me.'

'Well, Your Highness, while I hate to disagree…'

'Go on,' he invited, leaning forward.

'Well, then, if I answer in the affirmative, I'm essentially admitting to sidelining the members of her advisory cabinet who've travelled here to meet with you,' she pointed out sensibly. 'I would also be suggesting your time, which is, I'm sure, very valuable, has been wasted in these meetings about citizenship amnesties and debt forgiveness.'

'Because, despite the common-sense nature of those proposals, and the clear advantages to Ras Sarat in both of those arrangements, if you return to the Princess and tell her you don't like me, she won't go through with the wedding?'

Eloise pulled a face. 'It's not about whether or not I like you.' The last words were somewhat breathy. She cleared her throat. 'Your Highness.'

He ignored the addition of his title. 'Approve of me?'

'That's closer to the truth.'

'And what, pray tell, is your metric?'

'I'm sorry?'

'What tools are you using to assess my suitability?'

'I'm afraid it's not quite so scientific,' she said with another shrug. 'Ellie is my best friend in the whole world and has been for a long time. In truth, we're more like sisters; I know her better than anyone. I can't say what I'm looking for, but she deserves to be happy. And I don't know—I would like to know that you could make her happy, especially after all that she's been through.'

He ran a hand over his chin. 'I read about her fiancé.'

Eloise's face paled. It had been an awful time in Elana's life, which meant it had also been awful for Eloise. She swallowed, searching for what to say in response and decided there was nothing she could offer.

'She took his death hard?'

Eloise frowned. 'Of course, Your Highness.'

'They loved one another.'

She nodded, a small smile of nostalgia touching her lips. 'Madly.'

'I imagine she has mixed feelings about my proposal then.'

Eloise's eyes widened. 'I—' Damn it. She'd said too much. 'If Elana had decided against your offer, she would never have sent me.'

He was quiet, evaluating those words, and finally, he nodded once. 'And you also want this marriage to go ahead?'

How could she answer that without giving away the precarious circumstances the nation of Ras Sarat was in? The dire state of their economy and political system was something Eloise had no intention of revealing to this man. 'I make it a point to keep an open mind at all times.'

The flex of his brows intrigued her. A new reaction, one she hadn't witnessed yet.

'Besides being a loyal friend to the Princess, do you have any qualifications that makes you suitable for this role of trusted advisor?'

'The most important qualification is that she trusts me,' Eloise said softly. And that was saying something: Elana had frequently found herself surrounded by piranhas until Eloise had come to Ras Sarat. 'But I have other qualifications that she relies on, beyond this.'

'Such as?'

'Is it relevant, Your Highness?' Her eyes widened and cheeks glowed warm as she realised how she'd just spoken to him. 'I'm so sorry. That was unforgivably rude of me.'

'Direct, not necessarily rude. And in case you hadn't realised, I prefer frank conversations.'

'Nonetheless—'

'I'm not interested in your apology.'

He crossed his arms, drawing—and holding—
her attention on his broad pectoral muscles. He
wore the traditional thobes of his country, loose
and crisp, but now, they showed a hint of the defi-
nition she'd observed in photographs online, pic-
tures of him at events overseas, when he'd worn
western clothes and his body had been more discernible. Her mouth went dry. She reached for
a water glass before realising it belonged to the
previous occupant of her chair.

The Sheikh stood and now it was his height
that had her mouth drying out, and her eyes wid-
ening. He was easily six and a half feet, his frame
and physique things of great beauty, of rare, fascinating proportions, so she felt as though she
were in the presence of an ancient god. He moved
to an ornately carved table at the end of the room
and poured a fresh glass of water. Little pieces of
lemon and pomegranate bobbed on the surface,
and when he placed it in front of her, she caught
a hint of the fragrance.

'Thank you,' she murmured.

He dipped his head once, but rather than re-
turning to his own seat, he perched his bottom
on the edge of the boardroom table, close enough
that the fabric of his thobe draped a little over the
arm of her chair. Surreptitiously, she moved both
hands towards the water, out of the way of temptation. Temptation? A fine bead of perspiration

dampened the back of her neck and she looked away hurriedly, focusing on the exquisite view she had through the palace window, of a grove of fig trees, planted in perfect lines, hundreds of years old so they were each enormous enough to provide a significant canopy.

'Your qualifications,' he prompted, voice silky and mesmerising and so close she could almost imagine it wrapping around her, filling the spaces inside her chest.

She swallowed hard then replaced the water glass to the table, keeping one hand on it as though it were an anchor to reality and her obligations to Elana. It would be an easy thing to narrate her resume to this man, but something held her back.

'Why do you think I have any, besides my friendship with Ellie?'

'Your presence here would not be tolerated if it were friendship alone.'

Her brows lifted up. 'My presence here is *barely* tolerated,' she muttered, before realising how revealing that comment was. Heat flooded her cheeks and she hoped like heck she wasn't blushing.

'You weren't here yesterday; no one seemed to expect you today.'

He was very, very perceptive.

'Yes, Your Highness. I didn't travel with the contingent.'

'Why not?'

There were two answers to that, both valid: she hadn't been wanted by the negotiators, and they'd gleefully done everything in their power to come without her. But more importantly, she never flew anywhere if she could avoid it. Even the thought of it had her breaking out in a cold sweat. 'I drove,' she said after a beat.

'From Ras Sarat?'

'It's not so far.'

'It must have taken days.'

'Yes.' She rushed to fill the silence before he could push her further. For some reason, her fear of flying wasn't something she intended to share with this man. It was too personal, made her feel too vulnerable and raw. 'I like to take the scenic route whenever I can.'

His frown showed that he wasn't convinced, but he didn't push the matter further.

'As for my qualifications,' she said, 'I obtained a law degree from Oxford, and an economics degree from the London School of Economics.'

If he was surprised, he didn't show it. If anything, he appeared validated, as though he'd suspected her credentials.

'You studied with the Princess?'

'At high school and Oxford, yes.'

He mulled on that a moment and finally moved to the door, opening it. 'We will resume now.'

As if they'd all been waiting just on the other side for this exact moment, a line of delegates began to file back into the boardroom, and Eloise stood, moving quickly back to her own seat at the end of the table.

Their interaction had been strange and unfulfilling, and his rapid closing of their conversation had left her dejected and disappointed. Deflated. She'd been enjoying sparing with him and having his undivided attention. It was hard not to feel resentful now that he was addressing a room filled with others.

But then, he spoke, and the entire world seemed to tip completely off its axis. 'These negotiations should resume in a week's time. There is no purpose continuing at this stage.'

The chief diplomat from Ras Sarat spluttered and Eloise felt her pulse skyrocket for a whole other reason now. Had she said something wrong? Had she frightened him off? She'd come here to appraise his suitability, not ruin any hope of the marriage. Though Elana would never love him, she desperately needed this to work out.

'But, Your Highness, with all due respect, this is a very worthy match. While the finer details require some attention, surely you cannot intend to abandon the idea altogether?'

'Did I say that was my intention?' he asked coolly, addressing the portly man who'd responded.

'Well, no, but I cannot understand what other reason you could have for postponing—'

'Only that the Princess is yet to make up her mind. If she does not wish to marry me, arguing over import tariffs is a waste of all our time.'

'If Her Highness was not serious about the marriage, she would not have dispatched us so swiftly.'

'She would also not have sent an emissary to appraise my suitability as her husband,' Tariq said, and now Eloise *knew* her cheeks were as pink as they felt hot. All eyes in the room pivoted to her. 'A marriage is about more than trade arrangements and governmental cooperation. My own parents were an excellent example of the value of true partnership and cooperation.' Did anyone else in the room hear the underlying tension that accompanied that last statement? Eloise was conscious only of the Sheikh now, aware of every nuance and inflection in his voice. 'Her Highness has demonstrated great judgement in exercising caution despite the incentives for this wedding. But until Miss Ashworth is prepared to recommend the union to the Princess, it would be a waste of time to negotiate further.' He turned to Eloise with the full force of his attention now and all the air left her lungs in one crazy, wild whoosh.

'Therefore, Miss Ashworth and I will spend a week getting to know one another. I will make myself available to answer any of her questions. As the Princess will reside in Savisia, Miss Ashworth will also tour the palaces and familiarise herself with the culture of our country. At the end of that time, she will be better placed to offer her opinion to the Princess and, if suitable, we can resume negotiations then. Until that time, please, enjoy the hospitality of my palace, gentlemen.'

CHAPTER TWO

THE DIPLOMAT FROM Ras Sarat opened his mouth to reply but a man to the Sheikh's right beat him to it. 'His Highness has spoken.'

It was all that was needed to silence the rest of the room and move them towards the door. Eloise felt the barbed looks aimed in her direction as they filtered from the boardroom but she kept her back straight and pretended not to notice—ironic when she was such a keen student of human nature and expression. When they were almost all gone, she collected her folder and began to move towards the door herself, needing that fresh air and breathing space even more now.

'Not you, Miss Ashworth.'

Miss Ashworth. Hearing him address her in that way made her body tingle all over. 'Your Highness—'

'Yes, Miss Ashworth?'

Again? She dug her fingernails into her palms.

'Really, Your Highness, I don't think this is at all necessary.'

'Did I say anything you disagree with?'

He brow furrowed. 'Not exactly, but—'

'But?' He moved closer, his voice deep and mesmerising.

She swallowed, wondering if he felt the air crackling around them too. It was deeply inappropriate to reprimand a sheikh, particularly when acting as a representative for Elana, and yet she heard herself say, stiffly, before she could stop herself, 'I suppose a little notice of your intention wouldn't have gone astray.'

'I'm not in the habit of consulting anyone about my decisions.'

'Evidently.'

'Is that a mark against me already?'

Her lips quirked and again, despite the fact she knew she should be exhibiting purely deferential behaviour, she said, 'Let's just say I'm not a fan of autocracy.'

His laugh was as unexpected as it was delicious. She stared at him, open-mouthed, the sound rich and raw and virile and mesmerising. She gripped the back of a chair for support, and it was just about the only thing holding her upright.

'Let me see if I understand you, Miss Ashworth.'

She couldn't bear it any longer. It was so seductive to hear what his voice and accent did to her very prim surname. 'Eloise, please,' she insisted, allowing the informality on the basis that this man was very likely going to marry her very dearest friend, which would make them… friendly. It was okay for him to use her first name, surely!

'Eloise.'

Uh-oh. Hearing him say her name was like falling into a warm lagoon—even more dangerously seductive than the way he'd rolled his tongue around 'Ashworth'. She tried to tamp down on the butterflies in her tummy, but they beat their wings frantically regardless.

'You have come here uninvited—'

'I was sent here by the Crown Princess of Ras Sarat,' she interjected sharply, before she could stop herself.

His eyes narrowed. It was obvious that he wasn't interrupted by anyone, ever, and Eloise was almost as shocked as he! She had had three years of being spoken down to, denigrated, disrespected, and yet she held her course with calmness and dignity—always.

'Unexpected even by your own delegation,' he continued as though she hadn't spoken, and she was glad he didn't react, because her interruption was a misstep she didn't intend to make again. 'Your purpose in being here is to appraise me as a suitable husband. To ascertain the likelihood of your princess's happiness if this marriage were to proceed. I have signalled that I will work with you to make your job easier, and yet you think I'm somehow being…autocratic?'

He was right. This was above and beyond, and it would indeed make it easier for her to advise Elana. Nonetheless, Eloise couldn't help ticking her head to the side and studying him a moment.

'Say whatever it is you are thinking, Eloise.' Was he doing this on purpose? That time, he almost seemed to slow down as he said her name, like he could taste it, like it was the most delicious thing he'd ever tried.

'Only that we were speaking for several minutes, and there was ample opportunity for you to perhaps discuss your intention with me so it didn't come as quite a surprise when you announced it to the room.'

'Would you have agreed?'

'Elana is relying on me. Trusting me.'

'So you would have agreed?'

'We'll never know, as you didn't ask me.'

'I'm asking you now.' His arms crossed over his chest and the room seemed to shrink, so she was aware of him, her, and the volume of air between them, every little cubic centimetre of atmosphere. Her ears popped as though she were ascending a hill far too fast.

'Isn't that a little like shutting the gate after the horse has bolted?'

His eyes widened at her colloquial expression, and she wondered if she'd gone too far. 'You're doing everything you can to avoid agreeing with me, but you know that I am right.'

Her jaw dropped. He *was* right, damn it. 'I don't think a week is necessary,' she muttered. 'Your Highness,' she forced herself to add.

'We're talking about a lifetime commitment.' He waved a hand through the air. 'Take a week. Once Her Highness agrees to this, there is no turning back, for either of us.' Again, there was that look in his face of apprehension, of doubt. She leaned forward, breath held, fascinated by him, by his mind, his thoughts. Far too fascinated than was wise. 'I'm sure you'd prefer to know, beyond a shadow of a doubt, that your advice to her has merit.'

He had her cornered. There was no way she could refuse his suggestion now.

'Fine,' she said with a small nod, and then, because she worried she might seem churlish, she forced a smile to her lips. 'Thank you.'

His own smile showed; he saw through the polite acceptance, but she barely noticed his cynicism. Her eyes were transfixed by the curve of his mouth, and the beauty it gave his chiselled, symmetrical face.

'My chief of staff will have your things moved to the palace.'

'The palace?' She gaped. 'That won't be necessary. I have a perfectly adequate hotel room in the city.'

'You are here to appraise your princess's future life, are you not?'

She bit down on her lower lip, nodding slowly.

'Then you'll come and stay at the palace. Live as she would live. It will be the best way to give qualified advice.'

Another excellent point, but she wanted to buck against it. But the room…the man…everywhere she looked, she was reminded of his power and importance, his political prestige. It was in his air, his manner, his assessing gaze. He was not a man to be argued with—not over details that barely mattered. 'If you're sure, Your Highness.'

His chuckle was softer this time, and slower, so it wrapped around her like tentacles of smoke, pulling her towards him even when she stayed perfectly still.

'I'm sure, Eloise. Come, my chief of staff will take you to a guest suite.' He moved towards the door, big and strong, his thobe billowing behind him. She could only watch, frowning, as he drew near the door then pulled it inwards. He turned to face her, their eyes locked, and the floor seemed to give way.

'Do not look as though I am about to feed you to a pack of wolves. I assure you, it's not necessary.'

'What was that all about?'

'Showing my future wife the kindness of respecting her decision-making process? Do you think I erred?' Tariq pushed his own best friend and trusted advisor, studying the man carefully. A view of the Savisian gulf glistened in the distance, the sun bouncing off the surface as it often did by day. Though never, Tariq remembered with a shiver, in his nightmares.

'Of course not. I did wonder, however, if you were having second thoughts?'

'No,' he denied sharply. After all, Tariq didn't have the luxury of second thoughts. Not after what he'd learned. His lips tightened at the memory of the conversation he'd endured five months earlier, a day after burying his beloved father. It was the kind of conversation one could never forget, words that had shaken him to the foundation of his core, changing every single thing he knew about life and his place in it. The indefinable sense of rightness to his position in Savisia, to his role as ruler, was suddenly awash, adrift on the very same turbulent ocean that had swollen and rocked his sleep for years.

'Your father never wanted you to learn the truth, my darling. He was adamant I could not tell you.'

Tariq had considered that. For as intrigued as he'd been by his mother's pronouncement, he was also unfailingly faithful to his father, and trusted his wishes implicitly.

'If this secret mattered so much to him to keep, perhaps you should hold it for a little longer?'

'I can't. His death changes things.'

Her worry had been obvious and Tariq, ever the protector, had hated seeing her upset. He'd crouched beside her, bracing for whatever was to come.

'What things?'

She'd pleated the fabric of her pale skirt, fingers working meticulously to form line after line after line. He'd watched the gesture, waiting, every cell in his body locked.

A sob had bubbled from his mother. Such a shocking sound, he'd been a child once more, afraid of the dark, of small spaces, afraid even of his own shadow at times. Those were irrational fears he'd overcome many years earlier, fears his father had helped him face and rise above. Now, he feared nothing, not even the march of time itself.

But his mother's sadness…

It was too much.

'Your burden is heavy. Tell me, what is it? I promise, it will change nothing, Mother. Nothing of importance.'

What a fool he'd been then! So arrogant, so self-assured. He hadn't understood that he was standing on a shifting piece of earth, that his place in Savisia was subject to any force that might exert itself, at any point. He'd crouched beside his mother as she relayed the truth of his birth to an unknown mother, in a foreign country. There'd been an accident when he was just a baby; he'd been badly hurt, his family—two parents and a brother—had died, leaving him alone in the world.

The Sheikh and his Sheikha had found him on a routine tour of the hospital. His father had not been the ruling Sheikh, but only the younger brother. There was no plan for him to inherit the throne and what they did in their private life was exactly that—private. Years of infertility had meant his mother had suffered miscarriage after miscarriage. She was broken-hearted, facing a childless life, and yet here was a baby, all alone in the world, who needed her, desperately.

'I loved you from the moment I saw you, darling, and I knew, somehow, that the woman who'd given birth to you would have been grateful, would have wanted me to take you, because I would always love you.'

Tariq's father had fought it. It went against his customs, his beliefs, and while within their country, adoption was legal and practiced in circumstances such as this—when it was merciful to take a child into your home and raise them, when there was no blood relative left who could take custody—it was not commonplace enough to believe that it was a path open to them, members of the royal family. Even second brothers had constant scrutiny to deal with.

But Tariq's mother had refused to leave him.

She'd insisted. And fought. And cried. And on the tenth day of their tour, the Sheikh had relented. They would care for him for one month, he'd suggested. Just a month, while he got back to good health and an alternative was found.

Of course, one month turned into three, and then a year, as the little boy from Spain smiled and laughed and hugged them when he cried, so they both fell completely in love and realised he was their son in every way that mattered. Their intent had been to move to a small village and live a quiet life, just the three of them, but fate had other ideas...

He was so like them, with his dark skin and black eyes, dimpled cheeks and intelligent, inquisitive nature. It was impossible not to feel that in all the way that matters, Tariq truly was theirs.

They could never have known that by bringing him home and passing him off as their son, they would one day foist an outsider onto the throne, that they were asking the country to accept someone originally of a wholly different nationality as their ruler. The bloodline, an ancient pride of all Savisians, had ended with his parents.

Tariq was an imposter.

But there was salvation: an idea that had come to him in the middle of the night, when he recalled something he'd learned in grade school. His country and Ras Sarat had, hundreds of years earlier, been one and the same. Lands and borders had shifted over time, alliances had ended, but the bloodline remained intact. The Crown Princess Elana was royal, and in her body flowed the ancient royal lines that mattered so much to his people. By marrying her, he could redeem himself and ward off any possible claim another party might make to the throne.

For though he was not, as it turned out, born to rule, he had been bred for it, and little else. He knew he was an excellent sheikh, and that was all that mattered.

His marriage to Elana must go ahead at any cost: even if that meant hand-holding Eloise around the kingdom for the next seven days to ensure his generous and common-sense proposal was accepted.

'I have no second thoughts,' Tariq reiterated with the will of iron for which he was renowned. 'The wedding makes sense. It has to happen.'

'Yes. And it doesn't hurt that your intended bride is utterly stunning, I suppose.'

Tariq considered that, trying to conjure a mental image of the Crown Princess. Only there was another pair of eyes that flooded his brain, wide-set and the creamiest, almond butter—brown with flecks of gold and thick dark lashes. A heart-shaped face with a dainty ski jump nose and a swanlike neck that was perfectly in proportion to her fine-boned, dainty body. Unlike his swarthy complexion, her skin was obviously creamy pale, though slightly tanned courtesy of her life in sun-drenched Ras Sarat. Her fingers had been so fascinating, her nails short and sensible but somehow…beautiful.

Eloise.

Even just her name had an effect on him, so he ground his teeth together, forcing his legendary focus onto the matter at hand.

He hadn't been with a woman since his father fell ill. His body was craving what he could not have—and it was abundantly clear that the very best friend of his future wife was not a suitable partner. Any and all fantasies from this point on were strictly forbidden.

Even if her Cupid's bow lips had drawn his attention as she'd gulped back water, and made him imagine them cupped with just as much enthusiasm around another, worthier vessel…

He bit back a curse and gripped the railing more tightly.

'Beautiful or not, she is royal, and she is available. Having met her once or twice, I know she's sensible and conversant in the ways of royal life.'

He shrugged. 'That's the beginning and end of my wish list.'

Jamil considered his friend a moment and then nodded. 'Then you should do everything you can to win over Miss Ashworth.'

Tariq didn't think about the fun he could have if he truly wanted to win her over. After all, he'd sworn he couldn't have her, so there was no purpose wondering just exactly what she'd sound like when he kissed her.

There was only a little over an hour between being shown to the most sumptuous suite of rooms she could possibly imagine, and a servant appearing at her door, asking her to come to meet with Tariq. She wasn't sure what she'd expected, but at the servant's arrival, her heart had leaped into her throat. She thought of the brief text message exchange she'd shared with Elana, and her friend's gratitude.

This is perfect, Lissie. You're such a good judge of character and a week gives you long enough to really come to understand him. I owe you so much for this.

Of course, that wasn't accurate. Elana had saved Eloise, and they both knew it. In high school, she'd been utterly miserable, and Elana had sensed that, had made her smile again, had helped her through the darkness of grief and displacement. They were true best friends in every way, always looking out for each other.

I could never let you marry a man I didn't approve of. I'm glad to have the opportunity to appraise him.

She added a 'fingers crossed' emoji, then slipped her phone into the deep pocket of her dress, falling into step behind the staffer. This was about Elana, and what was right for her, nothing else. Certainly not the buzzing in her belly at the thought of seeing the Sheikh again.

She turned her concentration to the building, forcing herself to admire the enormously high ceilings, carved from marble and stone, with gold leaf detailing at the top of each pillar, and then the sparkling white tiles beneath them, marble as well, with a vein running through them that looked like silver. She ached to stop walking and take a closer look, to chase a vein with a fingertip and feel it pulse beneath her skin.

She adored history, and the ancient buildings of this part of the world were quite beyond compare. It wasn't just the grandiose furnishings and architecture she admired, but the older relics, too, like the tapestries that were hung with details of life millennia ago. She looked at them wistfully as they passed, making a mental note to come back another time and pore over them one by one, to understand this ancient, beautiful land.

The Royal Guard of Savisia was evident here, with armed guards in traditional uniforms standing sentry at each doorway. She passed twelve before the staff member leading her turned into another corridor, this one lined on one side with windows that framed a distant view of the sparkling ocean. Here, there were vases on either side of the corridor, with enormous arrangements of flowers that were native to this region. She breathed in the fragrance as they passed and was strangely homesick for Ras Sarat.

When had that country come to feel like home? When had she stopped craving the rolling fields of the Cotswolds, the sound of bees buzzing over the blackberry vines in spring, the feel of milky sun on her skin and late-afternoon rain, drizzling all around? She couldn't say, only that while she still loved England, it was very firmly a part of her past now, rather than where she felt she belonged.

Perhaps that old adage was right: home is where the heart is, and to all intents and purposes, her heart was with Elana. She had no family left of her own. Her parents had died, her great aunt had passed. There was no one else.

Just Eloise. She and Elana were kindred spirits in that way.

Which was why she had to get this right.

It was a huge responsibility, but she knew Elana, and she knew what she wanted in a partner—what she deserved. Not love, because that wasn't what Elana wanted, but respect, happiness and similar life outlooks that would make sharing the rule of both countries easy. She also knew the dire straits of the Ras Sarat economy, and how much pressure was on Elana's young shoulders, so if there was any way of making this work, Eloise was determined to see that happen.

With renewed purpose, she followed the servant all the way to an enormous pair of doors, framed on either side by floral arrangements at least as tall as she was.

The servant knocked, and Eloise waited, trying to ignore the way her stomach was somersaulting.

It was no use.

As soon as the doors opened inwards, and she saw the stunning room, with Sheikh Tariq in the centre, her heart slammed into her rib cage and her knees felt weak. It was an effort just to smile at him, and she was sure the result was a travesty of tight-lippedness.

'Eloise.' She was half tempted to ask him to

revert to calling her *Miss Ashworth*. Anything to stem the strange sensation overtaking her body.

'Your Highness.' She dipped into a curtsey out of habit, then straightened.

'How is your accommodation?'

Her lips twisted. 'Beautiful, thank you.'

'Good.' He nodded, and there was something in his eyes that made her feel as though he genuinely cared for her comfort. She ignored that—it was all about Elana. As it should be.

'Are those the rooms Elana would occupy, as your wife?'

His eyes were loaded with speculation when they met hers. 'My wife will share my apartment,' he corrected. 'It's more than big enough for two, or more.'

She was so conscious of the thundering of her pulse, she wondered how he didn't hear it. The noise was loud enough to flood her ears.

Reminding herself she was here to find out as much as she could about this man, she forced herself to put aside her own peculiar reactions and do what this position required of her. 'More?' she prompted easily.

'Well, yes. Naturally children will be required.'

'Children, plural?' she prompted, something wistful twisting in her gut. Flashes of desires she'd pushed to the back of her mind a long time ago suddenly danced right in the centre of her

vision, so for a moment, all she could remember
was her fervent hope for a large family. As an
only child, she'd had a quiet childhood and hers
had been particularly lonely. She'd craved noise
and love and fun, all the idyllic notions she'd
conjured as she'd sat solitary, reading or colour-
ing. But then, her parents' vicious fighting had
overshadowed that, and Eloise had come to crave
solitude and silence—a life lived alone, without
the risk of pain her parents had seemed to delight in inflicting on one another, and splashing
back onto Eloise, on a daily basis.

'That would be my preference. I grew up without a sibling,' he said, after a brief pause. 'It is
a large burden to place on a child's shoulders.'

'What burden is that?'

'Inheriting the throne.'

She nodded thoughtfully. She'd heard Elana
make a similar remark often enough. She didn't
doubt it was the truth. But hearing it from this
man intrigued her—far more than it should have.
Frustrated by her ever-present curiosity, she told
herself she was only acting as an agent for her
friend. 'Do you resent it?'

'Not at all.' His response was swift.

'And yet, you feel it to be a burden?'

'It's a precarious position,' he said after a beat.
'Your friend and I are in the same scenario. There

is no spare, for either of us. Marriage, and children, is a sensible precaution.'

'So you'd want children quickly?'

'I wouldn't see any point in delay,' he said with a shrug, as though it barely mattered.

That gave her a moment's pause, and she couldn't say why.

'Is that a problem?'

'I can't speak for Ellie.'

'Isn't that why you're here?'

'To see for her,' she corrected with an involuntary smile. 'There's a difference, Your Highness.'

'Indeed.' He gestured to a banquet style table behind them. 'I presume you haven't eaten lunch?'

'In fact, I haven't had breakfast,' she said. 'I was late to the meeting this morning and didn't get a chance.'

'Then let's eat while we talk.'

Right on cue, her stomach gave an almost audible growl. She fell into step beside him, and at the table, he put his hands on a chair, pulling it back, dark eyes watching her intently, indicating she should take a seat.

Her heart had lodged firmly in her throat. She stared at him for a few seconds too long then moved to the chair, consternation rioting inside her at his gesture. The last thing she wanted was to move anywhere near that close to him. Steel-

ing herself for the inevitable, she approached
the chair warily, eyeing it, before sliding into it
quickly, her breath rushed as he eased the seat
into the table. As he went to move to his side,
his hand brushed her shoulder and a thousand
sparks ignited through her bloodstream, so her
eyes flew to his face, wondering if he'd felt the
same searing connection, the electric shock of
awareness.

He gave nothing away, and she felt like a fool
for such an obvious response.

He took the seat opposite, and despite the size
of the table, it felt far too intimate. It was absurd.
They were in a state dining room, and yet, the fact
they were alone made her all too aware of him as
a man, rather than a sheikh. Suddenly, she wished,
more than anything, that she had more experience
with men! A few dates in college, one semi-se-
rious boyfriend a couple of years ago, didn't exactly leave her with the sort of blasé attitude she
suspected would come in handy right about now.

It was simply the novelty of this, that was all.

'Do you think the Princess would prefer to
wait before starting a family?'

It was surreal to lurch from fantasising about
him one minute to imagining him married to her
best friend the next. She almost had whiplash at
the conflicting notions.

'With respect, I've told you, Your Highness, it would be indiscreet of me to speculate.'

'Shouldn't this go both ways?'

'Meaning?'

'You're here to learn what you can, but it occurs to me you can provide information about my prospective bride that I don't currently possess.'

'Wouldn't you prefer to get to know her in person?'

He shrugged nonchalantly. 'That will come.'

A shiver ran down her spine and she looked at the food, simply for something to do, as a distraction. Tariq changed gears, gesturing to the dishes and explaining each delicacy carefully, before easing back in his chair and watching her through hooded eyes.

She took a few scoops of various meals, then a sip of her drink, before she felt brave enough to meet his eyes again.

'Does it make you uncomfortable?'

Feeling utterly transparent, her eyes widened. 'Does *what* make me uncomfortable?'

'Talking about Elana.'

'Oh.' Relief rushed through her. 'Not talking about her, *per se*. But sharing her personal details and wishes, yes.'

'And yet, you expect me to bear my soul—'

'I expect no such thing, Your Highness,' she promised, instinctively shying away from the idea of that. This man's soul, she suspected, would be every bit as dangerously fascinating as his body and face.

'Then how can you advise your friend properly?'

'I don't need to understand all your inner secrets to know if you're capable of making her happy. It's enough to see that you're decent and kind.'

'These are the traits you value most?'

'What I value is beside the point. I'm only thinking of Elana.'

'Of course,' was his whip smart response. 'And this is what she's looking for in her marriage?'

'Isn't everybody?'

He pulled a face. 'That's quaint.'

'You're making fun of me?'

'Perhaps I am.'

'Why?'

'People get married for many reasons, some considerably more mercenary and cynical than you're suggesting.'

Her lips parted. 'You take a dim view of marriage?'

'I proposed to the Princess, didn't I?'

'Why did you?' she asked, the question one she posed to satisfy her own curiosity.

'As I said, with no siblings, the lineage is imperilled. Until my father died, that didn't seem so urgent. Now, I'm the last remaining Sheikh. A situation I intend to rectify.'

'I see.' She dug her fork into a chickpea and prune curry, the fragrances making her stomach clench. She tasted it, then moaned, as delightful flavours assailed her. 'This is wonderful,' she said quickly.

'You seem fixated on the issue of children,' he said, ignoring her rapturous praise for the food. 'Is there a reason for that?'

Her heart went into overdrive. 'Such as?'

'A reason you think this might be a problem for your friend?'

'A problem? No, nothing like that.' In truth, she knew Elana understood the necessity of children. But it would break her friend's heart to bear those children to a man other than her late fiancé. It was a grief Eloise hated knowing Elana would need to go through. 'We haven't discussed it in years,' she murmured. 'But Elana has, as you pointed out, the same motivation as you. I'm sure she'll be amenable to your schedule.' She took another bite of food, then a sip of water, before hastily adding, 'But I'm not committing her to that. Obviously, that's a conversation the two of you will have to have, if you decide—'

'I have decided,' he said, quickly. 'I want to marry her. The only remaining choice is hers.'

Something strange panged in Eloise's side. She

felt as though she were being pressed into with the sharp blade of a knife.

'Why Elana?'

'Why not?'

She pulled a face. 'You can just tell me if you don't want to answer a question, Your Highness.'

His smile was perfunctory. 'Our cultures have a long, entwined history. It makes sense.'

'Yes,' she said, wondering at the emptiness in her gut. 'It does.'

'But you are English. Do you find the idea of an arranged marriage strange? Unpalatable?'

'If you and Elana are in agreement, it hardly matters what I think.'

'Nonetheless, I'm interested.'

She pressed a finger into the rounded tip of her fork, steadying her nerves. 'What if you don't like my opinion?'

'It will change nothing about mine,' he said. 'Your opinion is exactly that—your thoughts.'

'Well, then, Your Highness, seeing as you asked, I find the idea of any marriage off-putting.' She lifted her glass from the table without drinking from it.

'Why?'

'I'm not sure. Probably because my parents' marriage was such a red-hot mess.'

'In what way?'

They were straying into territory that really

didn't matter, and yet she didn't point that out to him. 'They were miserable together. They fought all the time.' She smiled to hide the pain of those memories. 'They only stayed together because of me. I can't tell you how many times I found myself wishing they'd just put each other out of their misery and divorce. I must be one of the only children who's felt that way,' she said with a shake of her head.

'What did they fight over?'

'The air they breathed,' she responded sharply. 'Absolutely, unfailingly everything. They were so different; I can't believe they ever thought it would work out between them. My mother was a control freak—a lawyer, in fact—and incredibly unyielding about everything in her life. She was neat and fastidious and anxious. My father was a total hippy who couldn't hold a job for longer than a week. He was messy and drank alcohol until he was loud and silly—not that I realised that at the time. He would forget to do the jobs she'd asked him to take care of.' She tried to get control of her emotions, to push the heavy memories away. 'Anyway, they died a long time ago.'

'I'm sorry.'

She lifted her shoulders. 'I was sad, of course, but in some ways, I was also quite numb. Every day of my life felt like such a roller-coaster, their deaths was just another drop off the side. Does that make sense?'

He nodded once. 'I imagine you got in the habit of carefully guarding your emotions around them, so that you had some defence mechanism already in place when they passed away.'

Her eyes were saucer-like in her face when they lifted to his. It was the most succinct way of describing exactly what she'd felt. 'Yes,' was all she could say, though it was completely inadequate.

'And so you've decided to avoid marriage in case it turns out like theirs?'

The question brought her closer to what they'd been discussing, but she was off kilter, feeling raw and exposed by the things she'd just shared with him, memories she usually kept far from the surface washing over her now.

'I...haven't made any firm decision,' she said with a slightly haunted expression. 'But it's a moot point, anyway.'

'Oh?'

'I'm not seeing anyone,' she said, wondering if he heard the brittle tone to her voice.

'Why not?'

She lifted her brows. 'Is it a prerequisite?'

'I'm just curious.'

'Why?'

'Because you're here.'

She laughed softly. 'Gee, thanks.'

'That's not intended as an insult.'

She sighed. 'I work long hours,' she said after a pause.

'As an advisor to the Crown Princess?'

'Yes.'

'What other matters do you advise her on?'

She hesitated. The state of the Ras Sarat economy wasn't a secret, but Eloise felt disloyal to go into too much detail. 'A broad range,' she hedged carefully.

'And if she chooses to marry, will you accompany her here?'

The question was far more loaded than it should have been. Something inside her chest lurched and she found the vision of that future strangely barbed. 'I...couldn't say,' she said after a beat. 'It would depend on Elana's wishes.'

'It sounds to me like she relies on you a great deal. Will that end when she marries?'

'She'd have your advisors, Your Highness. And you.'

'And yet she'd also have her hands full, adapting to life here, and as my Sheikha. Your support would no doubt be invaluable.'

'If she felt that way, of course I would accompany her,' Eloise agreed finally, wondering why it felt like she was inking a deal with the devil. Something was warning her that she should keep her distance from this scenario, that for all she wanted to serve and help Elana, her own needs might come into conflict with those goals.

She didn't like that feeling.

For as long as she could remember, she and Elana had been on parallel tracks. She didn't like the idea of coming to a point where she could no longer serve her friend. And why shouldn't she come to Savisia? What difference would it make where she lived? It was a question she couldn't answer, but she knew, on some intuitive level that it *did* make a difference, and she suspected the man opposite was the beginning and end of that reason.

CHAPTER THREE

'IT'S SO MUCH bigger than I realised,' Eloise said, staring down the hallway at the palace and then, at the man beside her. 'Are you sure you have time for this?'

'This wedding is of the utmost importance to me. You have my full and undivided attention for the next seven days. Starting with a tour of the palace.'

Her eyes flared wide, as they often did, and he felt a strange rush inside him. Desire. He'd stopped pretending he didn't recognise the feeling around the time she first tasted the chickpea curry. Her eyes had fluttered shut, her lips had swollen and parted, and she'd made a noise that was, oh, so similar to what he'd envisaged she might sound like if he were to kiss her. He'd found it almost impossible to think straight from that moment on. He'd stumbled through the rest of the meal, giving far too much attention to the full sweep of her lips, the curve of her breasts, the gentle movements of her hands, so he'd been as hard as a rock when their coffee had been cleared away. Grateful for his generous thobe, he'd suggested a tour in the hope the historical detail of the palace would take the edge off his physical awareness.

The only problem was that Eloise Ashworth was clearly a history buff. Every room they entered enticed such a delighted, cooing response that if anything, his awareness of her was growing by the minute.

It was...unexpected.

Reminding himself he'd had months of abstinence, he assured himself that he could slake his needs with another woman and return to the status quo tomorrow. Only...the idea left him cold. There was no woman he could think of in that moment that he wanted in his bed as he did Eloise.

And she was one woman he absolutely, definitely couldn't touch. His marriage to Princess Elana was the insurance policy he desperately needed. Through her legitimate place on the throne of Ras Sarat could he stave off any future challenges to his own rule. Such a challenge would not be based in law—technically, the fact that Tariq had been legally adopted meant he was conferred with the same rights as a biological child, in this instance that made him the heir to the throne. But something theoretical was not necessarily the case in reality and he couldn't imagine the people of Savisia happily accepting a foreigner as their Sheikh—not without an added legitimisation of his place on the throne, such as marriage to the Crown Princess of Ras Sarat.

Desiring his future wife's best friend was a recipe for disaster. Grinding his teeth together, he nonetheless allowed himself to move closer under the guise of gesturing to one of the tapestries that adorned the walls in the morning room.

'My mother uses this space to entertain,' he said. 'She likes the decorations.'

'So do I,' Eloise murmured. 'These tapestries are stunning. How old are they?' She spun around, perhaps not realising how close they were now standing, and she very nearly bumped into him.

Her lips parted and warm breath pressed to his cheek, courtesy of the face that was tilted to his. 'I—'

He knew he should say something to take the awkwardness out of their situation, but he didn't want to. He liked watching the expressions flitting across her face, showing that her own awareness of him was distracting her, making her contemplate something that they should both assiduously avoid.

'You?' he prompted, and with the spirit of the devil stirring, he leaned forward, ever so slightly, so her eyes fluttered shut quickly. He stared at her face with surprise, as if just realising how beautiful she was.

He'd been attracted to her immediately, but in Tariq's experience, desire was never hung on one thing or another—he was just as likely to be drawn to a woman who made him laugh as he was a woman he found physically appealing. But Eloise was like a finely crafted doll, her features exquisite and somehow hauntingly fragile, so they stirred something quite protective and defensive in his chest.

Her throat shifted as she swallowed and before he could stop himself, he lifted a hand, his finger pressing to the base of her jaw, so her eyes skittled open and lanced his. But hers were heavy with her own needs, as though she were wading through desire just to be able to look at him. 'This is—'

He said nothing this time, only stared. Her pulse was racing beneath his fingertips. Whatever she might say, her body's response to his was obvious.

Which was, as a point of fact, an enormous problem. If his desire was one-sided, then he'd never dream of acting on it. It would have been easier to ignore her. Knowing she felt as he did made him want to rip the long, elegant dress from her body and take her right there on the ancient rug at their feet, to hell with who might interrupt them, to hell with anything.

Not since he was a teenager, and perhaps not

even then, had he felt so overcome by his physical needs. Even with his monumental control at play, Tariq wasn't sure he could keep this situation in check. Nor that he even wanted to.

'Your Highness.' Her breathy words were a plea and God help him, hearing her call him by his title made his already rock-hard arousal strain painfully against his pants. 'I think…'

He waited, staring at her, heat buzzing between them, the air thick with their breaths and awareness, with a mutual, desperate need. 'You are very beautiful.'

It was not something he'd intended to say.

Her eyes fluttered shut but she stayed where she was, dangerously, tantalisingly close. And then, of its own volition, his hand lifted, finding a stray clump of dark hair and tucking it behind her ear.

'Your Highness.' Now her voice shook a little. 'Stop.' But she whispered the last word, and if anything, swayed forward, so their bodies touched and electricity arced frantically around the room, lightning striking in response to the physical contact. 'We can't—'

'No,' he agreed, not moving. 'We can't.' His hand dropped to her chin. He'd meant to pull his hand away, but it sought her flesh, desperate to touch, to feel her skin for himself, and it was every bit as soft as he'd predicted. Like a rose petal on a dewy morning. He bit back a curse.

She lifted her face to his, and his hand moved, not down, as he'd intended, but higher, so he could trace the outline of her lower lip. Her breath released in a shuddering exhalation, and then her teeth pressed to her lip, her eyes clinging to his, swirling with a need he well understood—it was the same need rocking him to his foundations.

'It's crazy,' she whispered, eyes huge, but still she stayed where she was.

She was exactly right. He felt temporarily insane, made so by the depth of physical desire flushing his system.

'I intend to marry her,' he said, as if to agree with Eloise.

The colour drained from her cheeks and she blinked at him, as if the words didn't make sense.

'And yet,' he muttered, hating himself, hating her too, just because something about her was capable of making him want things he absolutely shouldn't.

'Your Highness,' she whispered plaintively.

'Perhaps you should call me Tariq.'

She shook her head, dislodging his thumb. His hand dropped to their sides, and captured hers, fingers weaving together.

'I can't. That's too…real.'

He understood. They were in an alternate reality, or at least one adjacent to the real world, but boundaries still mattered.

'I've never met anyone like you,' she said, and something ancient and primal soared in his chest. 'I don't usually feel...'

'What do you feel?' he asked, frustrated, when she trailed off into nothing.

'Isn't it obvious?'

His pulse slammed through his body. 'I want to kiss you.'

She groaned, shook her head slightly, but then, she was lifting up onto the tips of her toes, her mouth a mere inch from his. 'This is so wrong.'

She was right. It was crazy and wrong and also utterly unavoidable. Being alone with her made this inevitable—perhaps they should have realised that before now and avoided a situation like this. But they were here, and it was impossible to think they'd be interrupted. Not here, not now.

'Do you want me to stop this?'

Her smile was sardonic. 'Do you think you can?'

His eyes flared at her acknowledgement. She too felt the inevitability of this. 'No.' And he dropped his mouth then, closing the distance and kissing her as though his life depended on it. She tasted like coffee and almond essence, and he plundered her mouth desperately, seeking more of her, all of her. His hand lifted to the back of her head, cradling her, so he could steady her for his thorough inspection, his tongue flicking hers at first before taking complete control of her mouth, revealing every part of her for his delight. His body was so much bigger than hers, he felt he practically enveloped her as they stood like that, her own slight curves moulded to his frame, her breasts softly crushed to his torso, so he growled into her mouth, his free hand lifting to stroke the side of her stomach before moving higher, his fingers finding the underside of her breast and running over it possessively, hungrily. There was nothing languorous about his touch; he needed her with a ferocity that could have terrified him, and his kiss was a signal of that.

She kissed him back with the same fervent need though, her breathing frantic, her body writhing against his, as if trying to *feel* more of him than their clothes allowed.

He swore, desperate for more, reaching down and finding the expansive fabric of her skirt, pulling it up, and up and up, over her legs, until he held it bunched in his hands and he could reach around and cup the silk of her underpants, pushing her against his rock-hard arousal.

She whimpered into his mouth as she rolled her hips, and he took her lead, pushing himself against her, thrusting as if he could somehow miraculously be inside her moist warmth. He swore once more, and the hand that was cupping her buttocks moved between her legs, pushing aside her underpants so he could press a finger to her sex before striking inside of her.

She cried out, breaking their kiss only so she could drop her head backwards, her face scrunched with pleasure as her tight, moist muscles spasmed around him, gripping him so tight it was impossible for a little seed not to spill from him in response to these sensations.

'I want you,' he growled, stating the obvious, moving his mouth to her throat and sucking the flesh there, while his fingers moved between her legs and her voice grew higher in pitch and far more urgent. 'I know this is wrong and we will both regret it, but I cannot tell you how much I don't care right now. Say you want me too.'

He didn't need her to say it. He could *feel* it. He knew it with every cell in his body, and yet he wanted her to admit as much, to speak the words. Too much was at stake for both of them, for him to follow his instincts alone.

Her crescendo was building, fiercely wrapping around them, so he rode the wave with her, sucking her neck as he drove her over the edge of pleasure, her orgasm fierce and intense, her muscles convulsing around his fingers, her voice heavy in the air. He held her tight, his arousal desperately seeking entrance, needing her, needing to get this out of his system so he could return from the brink of insanity. He pulled his hand away purely so he could remove his clothes but in doing so, something between them shifted and she lifted her hands to her mouth, staring at him as though seeing him for the first time.

'Oh, my God,' she whispered, eyes clenched shut, not on a wave of pleasure now but one of comprehension. 'Your Highness, that was—' She turned her back on him, her slim shoulders shaking. 'I'm so sorry.' Her soft apology tore at something inside him.

'What for?' He moved to her, so they were toe to toe once more. His own desire had not abated.

'For letting that happen. For wanting it to happen. For standing here and basically begging you to make love to me.' She grimaced, her face paler than paper. 'That was a terrible, terrible mistake.'

It was the very last thing he wanted to hear. 'A mistake? Hardly.'

'You think not?'

'It's…inconvenient,' he said, choosing his words with care.

'Elana is my best friend,' she groaned. 'And I'm here to see if you're a good match for her. What am I meant to say? That you're a very smart, handsome guy who hits on any woman in his proximity?'

'That's not what this was,' he said quickly.

'Oh? Then what was it?' she demanded.

'I haven't been with a woman in months,' he clarified.

'That's even worse! So you would have had sex with me just because it's "been a while"?' All formality was, for the moment, lost. 'Even though my best friend is your future wife?'

His eyes narrowed, and just like that, his desire faded, leaving something hollow in its place. Tariq was known for many things, his black-and-white morality amongst them. 'She is not yet my future wife,' he reminded her, aware it was really only a technicality. 'Neither of us has officially agreed to the marriage.'

'But you *intend* to marry her,' Eloise muttered. 'If she'll have you, which she will, if I recommend it. Don't you understand? She trusts me! She's relying on me. I can't—I can't go back and tell her to marry someone that I've—if we've—'

He understood perfectly. Everything she was saying made perfect sense, he just didn't particularly like hearing it.

'Fine, it was a mistake,' he agreed with her first summation. 'It won't happen again.'

Disappointment that dulled her eyes. 'Good,' she whispered, running her hands down her dress, straightening it, pulling away from him. 'It *can't* happen again, Your Highness.'

'Then please, call me Tariq,' he said after a pause. 'You keep using my title and I have to tell you it leads me to want to rip every shred of fabric from your body and make you shout it from the rooftops.'

Her gasp was loud enough to split the room in two, the imagery as evocative to Tariq as it was to Eloise.

'Duly warned,' she said quietly. 'That can never happen again… Tariq.'

It was impossible not to envy him, and to marvel at his prowess, for not ten minutes after making her see stars, she was watching the Sheikh of Savisia speak to his mother as though nothing earth-shattering had taken place, whatsoever.

'I've always loved Ras Sarat,' the Sheikha murmured, her greying hair pulled up into a loose bun, intelligent eyes focused on Eloise, so it took all of her concentration not to blush. Surely her face showed exactly what had just happened? Damn it, she wished they hadn't met like this, but it had been unavoidable.

Tariq had insisted on walking Eloise back to her suite, where she'd intended to hide out for at least the next century, only the older regent had been sitting in a dappled courtyard they happened to cross through, and when she offered tea, Eloise knew it would have been very poor form to demur. Despite the fact tea was the last thing she wanted. Despite the fact she could barely think straight. Despite the fact her knees were wobbling and her breath rushing and her breasts tingling and her stomach in knots.

She plastered a smile to her face, forcing herself to sit demurely, to remember all of the etiquette lessons she and Elana had joked about over the years. Hands clasped in her lap, shoulders relaxed, feet crossed at the ankles.

'Do you travel there often?'

'Yes, in fact. It's where we took our honeymoon.' Something wistful crossed the older woman's expression and belatedly, Eloise recalled the recent passing of the Sheikh.

'I was sorry to hear about His Highness,' she murmured, aware of Tariq's eyes on her. Aware of them? Hyper-aware, more like. They burned her, lingering on her skin, tantalising her, mocking her, reminding her of what they could be doing, if only she hadn't panicked.

'It was a great loss.'

'I'm sure.'

'Did you ever meet him?' the Sheikha prompted.

'No, Your Highness. I didn't have that good fortune.'

'He was there quite recently.'

'He met with the Crown Princess, in fact,' Eloise said, with a nod. 'She always praised him.'

'My husband was an excellent man.' The older woman's eyes moved to Tariq, love obvious in their depths. 'And my son made him very proud.'

Eloise's heart skipped a beat. 'I'm sure.' The words, to her own ears, were slightly wooden, and she saw in the answering flicker of Tariq's lips that he heard and understood.

'Have you lived in Ras Sarat for long, dear?'

'A few years.'

'And what brought you to this part of the world?'

'Friendship, and occupation.' She wrinkled her nose. 'And a need for change, and perhaps the *umm ali.*'

The Sheikha smiled. 'One of my personal favourites.'

'I didn't have a sweet tooth until I tried it.'

'Our chef makes the best you've ever tasted.' She turned to Tariq. 'Will you have some made for Eloise?'

'Would you like some, Eloise?' he asked, his voice hinting at a double entendre, so her stomach twisted and she sent him a furious glance. How could he make light of this? She ground her teeth together, offering a saccharine smile.

'I shouldn't. I know it's not good for me.'

'Sometimes it's good to be bad.'

'But the consequences,' she added, flicking a tight smile at the Sheikha, who was oblivious to the undercurrent of tension.

'It's your choice,' he said with a lift of his shoulders, his eyes sparking with hers to the point she couldn't bear it.

She stood abruptly, her trademark grace nowhere in sight as she quickly came behind her chair and gripped the back.

'Excuse me, Your Highness,' she said, ignoring the Sheikh. 'I promised the Princess I'd check in with her, and I'm overdue. Do you mind?'

'Of course not, dear. Thank you for taking the time to speak with me. I enjoyed meeting you.'

Her heart gave a strange clutch. 'And I you.'

She turned without another glance in Tariq's direction. She couldn't look at him. She had the strangest feeling that she would cry if she wasn't very, very careful.

'Eloise.' His voice arrested her as she passed through the doors that led to the inside of the palace.

She dug her fingernails into her palms and stood perfectly still, without turning to face him.

'You forgot this.'

Now she tilted her face, just enough to see him holding her handbag.

Inwardly, she groaned, forcing herself to nod her thanks. But when he was close enough that only she could hear him, he murmured, softly, 'You're running away from me.'

Her eyes flared wide and she made her escape while she still could, legs trembling all the way back to her suite of rooms.

CHAPTER FOUR

'Tariq!' She stared at him, heart kicking into overdrive, mind racing at his sudden appearance at her suite. 'It's almost nine o'clock.'

'Yes, it's late. I had a meeting. But as you haven't eaten, I've come to collect you.'

'How do you know I haven't eaten?'

He lifted his brows. 'I asked.'

'Why?'

'I'm not in the habit of explaining myself to anyone in Savisia.'

It was so arrogant she almost laughed. 'Why don't you give it a shot?'

He didn't react, but she felt the amusement humming through him and delighted in that. She liked making him smile. She liked… Danger sirens blared, and she heeded them, gripping the door more tightly.

'You're my special guest. I made plans for our dinner.'

'Together?' she squeaked.

'Unless you are afraid to be alone with me?'

'I'm not afraid.'

'Then you are a fool,' he muttered, a rueful expression on his face. 'We're playing with fire, you know.'

'I'm not playing with anything.'

'We'll see.'

'And even if that were true, isn't it all the more reason for us to keep our distance?'

'I can't do that.'

'Why not?'

'I've announced to my cabinet and yours that I am spending the next week with you. I intend to see that through.'

'But surely this afternoon—'

'Changes nothing,' he said flatly. 'It can't.'

'I know, but—'

'You still want to get to know me, don't you? To see if you should recommend this marriage to Elana or not?'

She closed her eyes, caught between a rock and a hard place. 'Yes,' she admitted, finally, grudgingly.

'Then come and share a meal with me.'

'You make it sound so simple.'

'Isn't it?'

It should have been. After all, what they'd shared was meaningless, in the scheme of things. He wasn't to know that her experience with men was so limited. Clearly, his knowledge of female anatomy was first rate, undoubtedly garnered through extensive experimenting. So why couldn't they just forget the kiss, and everything else, and focus on the reason she'd come to Savisia in the first place?

'Fine,' she said with a huff. 'But don't even think about touching me.'

'I can't promise that,' he murmured. 'But I won't act on those thoughts unless you ask me to.'

Her lips parted and she groaned. 'Why are you doing this?'

'What am I doing, Eloise?'

'Flirting with me.'

'I'm simply being honest.'

'Well, don't do that either,' she snapped. 'At least, not about…us. I can't even think about this,' she said, pointing from his chest to hers, 'right now.'

'Then I envy you.'

She growled. 'I'm serious. You might be master of all you survey, but don't think I won't stomp on your foot if you keep saying things like that.'

'Stomp on my foot?'

'Sure. Or knee you somewhere significantly more painful.'

He laughed, a deep, husky sound that made her blood bubble and overheat. 'But then, I'd have to defend myself.'

She shouldn't ask. She really shouldn't ask. 'And how would you do that?'

'I suspect it would involve your wrists being pinned to a wall, for a start.'

Just the suggestion made her bones melt. 'Damn you,' she snapped, but the words were breathy, lacking any true sense of outrage.

'Relax. I won't touch you. I won't flirt with you. Tonight, I will be on my best behaviour.'

She tried to ignore the shearing sense of disappointment, but it was impossible. She bit into her lip and finally nodded. 'Okay. Dinner. And only because I'm starving.'

'I'm flattered.'

She scowled. 'Somehow, I think your ego's probably sufficiently supersized to survive a few home truths from me.'

He laughed and again, her body reacted with a sharp ping of desire. She forced herself not to reveal it.

'You know, your reaction makes me think you don't get kissed anywhere nearly often enough.'

She gaped. 'I'm not having this conversation with you.'

'Why not?' he asked, gesturing for her to step out into the corridor. Begrudgingly, she did so, eyes firing to his.

'How about, because it's none of your business?'

'Is it a big deal?'

She rolled her eyes. 'No.'

'A state secret of some sort?'

'No.'

'So?'

'You really want my kissing resume?'

'Not a full resume,' he said with a tilt of his head. 'More of an overview.'

'And do I get the same information about you in return?'

'Are you sure you'd like it?'

'I think I'd be neglectful not to ask,' she said after a pause. 'After all, you're hoping to marry my very best friend.'

'Does my sex life impact on my suitability as a spouse?'

'It might.'

'Fascinating. How so?'

'I don't know. Just how active is your sex life?'

'Currently? Until this afternoon, I'd say it was non-existent.'

She stopped walking, lips parted, floundering. 'That's not fair.'

He lifted his hands in a gesture of surrender. 'You asked for the truth, though.'

'Yes, well, could you try to speak it in a less inflammatory fashion, please?'

He dipped his head. 'Your wish is my command.'

Something twisted in her gut. She was having *fun*. Despite the forbidden nature of what they'd shared, despite the lurching feeling that she'd taken a serious misstep and was letting down the one person on earth she thought of as family, she couldn't deny that sparing with Tariq was a highly enjoyable activity.

He stopped walking, and two servants opened a pair of doors. She stepped inside, looking around in a cursory manner until it became apparent that he'd brought her to a courtyard, though not the same one she'd seen that afternoon, with his mother. This one had a very beautiful fountain on the edge and a sunken seating area with a fire pit at the centre. Though the day had been warm, the evenings were cool, thanks to the desert air, and she moved towards the fire on autopilot.

'My father's death changed things for me,' he said quietly, close behind her, so with her back to him, she allowed herself the indulgence of closing her eyes, of listening to him, hearing his words, allowing them to weave through her soul. 'I haven't been with a woman since we buried him.'

Five months. All the breath left her lungs as she began to understand why he'd found it so hard to control himself around her. She was probably the first woman he'd been alone with since then. No wonder he'd struggled to keep a distance. After all, his libido was somewhat legendary. What exactly was her excuse?

'You must have loved him very deeply.'

'Yes.'

'And before he died?' she whispered, afraid that he was right: that she didn't want to know.

'Why do I think you already have the answer to that?'

'Because you're a smart man.'

'Yet you want to hear it from me?'

'Yes.'

'I enjoy the company of women, and it is not something I've ever been short of.'

She forced herself to turn then, to face him, and caught him in a moment of reflection, his eyes on the flickering flames.

'Have you ever been in love?'

The question had his eyes flickering to hers, then away again. 'No.'

She frowned. 'Why not?'

He hesitated, and she felt a weight in that silence, a consideration that spoke of thoughts he was choosing not to express. 'I can't answer that.'

'Because you don't know?'

'Because it's too personal.'

She compressed her lips, trying not to show how much that hurt. But it did, and even Eloise was surprised. After all, why should she care so much?

'So these women you enjoy the company of are what?'

His lips curled. 'Surely you're familiar with the concept of lovers?'

She gasped, his raw honesty startling and confronting, hateful and…so deliciously seductive. She turned her back on him, lifting her hands to the flames and pretending to warm herself.

'You're deliberately baiting me.'

'Am I?'

'I meant to ask if you dated them, or simply took them to bed…but on reflection, I don't think I need to know. Just tell me that when you marry Elana, you'll be faithful to her.'

The silence that hung between them was heavy and she wondered if he could hear the rushing of her blood, the throbbing of her strangely erratic heart.

'I take vows of any kind very seriously.'

'I'm glad.'

He came to stand beside her. 'Your turn.'

'What for?' She blinked up at him with wide-eyed innocence.

'Your, what did you call it? Kissing resume?' His eyes fell to her lips and she knew that if she were being completely honest with him, she'd tell him there'd only ever been one kiss that mattered, one kiss that had the power to reshape the entirety of reality and gravity and cosmic power.

But instead, she lifted her shoulders in what she hoped would pass for nonchalance and pursed her lips. 'I don't keep an exact count.'

There was no humour on his face now, and the intensity of his gaze made her breath shallow. 'Have you ever been in love?'

She reached for a blasé answer, but something about his intelligent, assessing eyes and the stars that shone so brightly overhead, and the crackling of the flames in the pit in front of them, made her feel that their conversation was taking place out of time and space. She shook her head almost without realising it.

His eyes skimmed hers, reading her. 'Is that so?'

'You think I'm lying?'

'I'm simply surprised.'

'Why?'

'You're beautiful and fascinating. Surely you have men beating a path to your door.'

'Even if that were true,' she said with a small shake of her head, 'attracting the interest of men is not quite the same thing as welcoming it. Or being in love.'

He was too shrewd, too seeing. 'And you don't welcome male attention.'

She turned away from him. 'I think I'll take a leaf out of your book. That's too personal.'

'Is it?'

She dipped her head. 'This whole conversation is absurd,' she said, after a beat. 'I told myself I wouldn't let this happen again, but here you are, weaving the same spell around me as you did this afternoon. I can't do this.'

She turned to walk away but he caught her hand, pulling gently, drawing her back to him, and now the tears she'd been fighting all afternoon felt dangerously close to the surface.

'She's my best friend,' Eloise whispered, lifting her free hand and pressing it to his chest. 'She's more than that. Elana is the only family I have. I would never do anything that would hurt her. Please, you have to respect that.'

His eyes bore into hers and she held her breath, waiting, needing, wishing, but their souls were speaking now, making a pact that went beyond her plea and his promise.

'You're right,' he said quietly, releasing her hand and taking a step back. 'I'm sorry.'

His apology was the last thing she'd expected. It pulled at something inside of her. Emotions that she had no experience with were zipping out of control now.

'Your loyalty is a quality I greatly admire. It was wrong of me to ask you to betray her.'

'To be fair, I was pretty complicit,' she couldn't resist saying, the words brittle, laced with shame. 'I shouldn't have let things go this far. If you were not her friend, then things would be different, but you are. I understand.' He lifted her hand to his lips and kissed it, but quickly, chastely, with no promise of anything further. Her heart developed a fissure right down the centre, but she told herself it was with relief and gladness.

'Okay,' she forced a smile to her mouth but it felt wooden and heavy. 'Thank you.'

His eyes glowed when they met hers. 'Let's eat.'

For three days, the Sheikh was on his best behaviour and Eloise told herself she was glad. Glad he was being businesslike and professional, glad he delegated some of the sightseeing to minions, glad that he kept a respectful distance from her at all times.

Glad that he didn't touch her or kiss her or even look at her as though he wanted to.

Glad that her evenings were kept free, except for one thing: when she was alone, he was in her thoughts, her mind, his phantom touch on her body, his lips on her lips, his taste in her mouth, his touch in her body, so she was almost mindless with exhaustion and distraction by her fourth morning in Savisia.

Eloise had been so sure that she wasn't interested in a relationship with anyone—what were the chances of the first man who got under her skin and made her question everything being a man who'd proposed marriage to her best friend?

A hysterical laugh bubbled inside of her, so she reached for her cup of tea, still piping hot, and sipped it, glad for the way it scalded her throat a little. His marriage with Elana would be purely one of convenience. For Elana, it was essential to boost her country's flagging economic and political position in the region. But what about Tariq? Why had he chosen Elana? She frowned, contemplating that.

Why did he need children so desperately *now*? He was young and virile, and while he was the last of this line of the Savisian royal family, at thirty, and in good health, it was hard not to think he had at least a few years. Years in which to find a bride and marry for love. To marry someone he cared about, not just another princess.

But that wasn't why she'd come here.

Eloise's job was to see if she could recommend the marriage. She thought now of everything she knew about Tariq, everything she'd known before arriving and everything she'd heard and seen since, and her heart gave a funny little pang.

His reputation had preceded him. He was well-regarded by absolutely everyone. Not a single person could fault him. He was respected, liked, admired, but in person, it was impossible not to recognise his many personal charms, not to be overwhelmed by them. Elana would not likely love him—her heart had been lost when her fiancé had died—but she would like him. She would really like him, and she'd enjoy being married to him. They were definitely compatible.

Eloise felt a tick in the centre of her chest. She ignored it. She had to focus on Elana now, not her own stupid, selfish desires and wants. Not the little fantasy she'd developed in which Tariq was a normal man and she was not the best friend of the woman he'd sought to propose marriage to.

With a groan, she banged her palm against her forehead, wanting to push all thoughts from her mind that weren't relevant, but they pursued her, rushing through her, pulling at her, so eventually, she gave up, deciding on a walk to clear her mind instead.

The palace was incredibly beautiful. Beyond anything she'd ever seen before, in fact. It wasn't simply the grandiose nature of the architecture—and it *was* impossibly grand—but also the way the palace had been designed, at some long ago point in time, to make the most of nature's bounty. In one direction, large curved windows framed striking views of the desert, the vastness making one feel inconsequential and vital at the same time. In the other direction, the ocean shimmered, the capital city a testament to modernity with glass-and-steel monoliths cutting like blades through the crisp blue sky. The palace was surrounded by lush, green gardens—a testament to genius aquaculture, the diversion of a nearby river offered year-round irrigation, making for dense, immaculate lawns. The trees were mostly natives to this region or those with similar temperatures, and prospered in the climate: junipers, date palms, figs. Strong and sturdy, reminding her, quite suddenly, of the Sheikh of Savisia. She stopped walking abruptly, staring at one of the trees as her breath quickened in her throat.

He was so completely of this land, it was a part of him, and he of it. He'd proposed marriage because it was his duty to marry, and he would marry for that same reason. He would marry Elana because it made sense.

She forced her feet to move, taking her step by step towards the wide doors that led to one of the many courtyards surrounding the palace. She'd explored extensively in the last few days and knew this was one of the ways she could access the gardens. The sky was turning, fading from the brightness of the afternoon to the magical light of the dusk, the stars beginning to peep down on Savisia, the desert birds issuing their lilting night cries. She inhaled, the fragrance familiar yet different, so like Ras Sarat, and yet so unique, quite unlike anything she'd ever known before.

Her hands trailed a nearby rose bush and an errant spike caught her finger. She lifted it to her face for closer inspection, noting the perfect droplet of blood that seeped out. With a grimace, she kept walking, past the rose bushes, to a large field of citrus trees that reminded Eloise of an army—each tree stood strong and proud, heavy with leaves and blossoms, preparing for the winter when fruit would burst on these limbs, weighing them down, dragging them closer to the earth. She imagined the delight of a sun-kissed orange eaten here. She imagined peeling the skin and lifting the quadrants to her lips, tasting the sweet flesh as juices ran down her fingers. She imagined Tariq taking her by the wrist and drawing her sticky, citrus scented fingers to his mouth, licking each one, eyes locked to hers, mesmerising, heavenly.

She gasped, pushing the errant thought from her mind.

But that wasn't enough. The strength of her thoughts had conjured him—or so it seemed to Eloise, who was startled from her X-rated thoughts by the sound of hooves thudding across the ground, and a moment later, the sight of Tariq astride a magnificent stallion, black with rippling muscles and a mane that had been expertly braided.

She could only stare as he made his way across

the field beyond the citrus trees. He sat straight on the horse's back, his frame impossible to mistake for any other man's, his expert command of the beast never in question. He rode as though he and the horse were one, their thoughts shared, their purpose unified. She lifted a hand to her lips, knowing this image would be burned into her brain for life. The perfection of it, the rightness, the fascinating, undeniable sensuality.

A low groan formed in the base of her throat. It was silent. A thought, more than anything, but he responded as though she'd shouted his name, his head turning, eyes pinpointing her precisely, exactly, so she froze to the spot, fingers pressed to her lips, as she'd been fantasising about only moments earlier.

Everything shimmered. The horizon, the sky, the horse's mane, every cell in her body seemed to tremble and glisten. Without hesitation, he tugged on the horse's rein, and the beast responded instantly, changing course, tacking away from the open field, feet kicking up, moving faster, with an urgency that matched the fast flowing of her blood, until Tariq was riding through the citrus grove, cutting a path directly to her.

CHAPTER FIVE

SHE COULDN'T MOVE. Her legs were divorced from her body. She stayed where she was, trying desperately to rally her thoughts, to remember that she was there to serve her friend, not her own selfish, and terrifying, desires.

It was just that she hadn't seen him properly in days. It heightened everything, making her awareness of him as much a fundamental property as light and air.

'Eloise,' he said with a dip of his head, the words coated with something gruff and raw.

The horse expelled a breath, then studied her with undisguised curiosity, so she smiled because the beast really was a mirror of its owner.

'Your Highness.'

His eyes narrowed and belatedly she recalled his warning about the use of that title. More precisely, she remembered what he'd said it made him want to do, and her pulse tripped into a chaotic rhythm.

'I was just exploring the garden,' she murmured, gesturing to the trees. 'It's such a beautiful evening, I wanted to get out of the palace for a while.'

She was babbling. The silence stretching between them made her need to fill it—an uncharacteristic gesture for someone who was usually self-possessed.

'Your horse is beautiful,' she added.

'I don't think Bahira would appreciate that adjective.'

'He's too alpha for beauty?' she asked, a smile tickling the corners of her lips.

'Oh, absolutely.'

'Handsome? Buff? Striking?'

'Tough,' he corrected, amusement in his tone.

'Well, he's lovely.'

This time, Tariq lifted a single, thick brow, then grinned, so her heart stammered.

'Anyway,' she took a step backwards, 'I won't keep you.'

'You're not.'

Her expression was laced with irony, yet she didn't move. 'Do you…ride often?' She cringed as soon as she'd asked the question. She sounded like a love-struck teenager.

'Yes.'

She took a step backwards. She really needed to leave.

'Does the Princess ride?'

Eloise told herself she was glad he'd brought up Elana. Every time she could remember why she was here, the better. 'She knows how to, but it's not her favourite pastime.'

'Oh?'

'She was thrown, as a child. She's never got over it. She was made to continue riding, after that, but it was a pretty traumatic experience for her.'

His eyes roamed her face. 'And you?'

She swallowed, her throat thick and dry. 'I… No. I've never learned.'

'Have you ever been on a horse?'

She shook her head.

'Why not?'

She pulled a face. 'I grew up in England.'

'Last I checked, horses existed there too.'

She laughed. 'Sure, but not for people like me.'

'Meaning?'

'My parents didn't have much money. They were aristocratic, but like so many in their position, death taxes and the high cost of maintaining big country homes drove them into debt, Your High—Tariq.' But now, his name felt like a caress. All she could remember was how she'd whispered it into his mouth, begging him to hold her closer, tighter, begging him to take her. It pushed all thoughts from her mind for a moment, so she had to concentrate to grab hold of what she'd been saying. 'And horse riding is an expensive hobby.'

'You went to an excellent school.'

She glanced up at him. 'How do you know—?'

'You met the Princess at school,' he reminded her. 'And I know where she attended. The fees are not cheap.'

'No,' she agreed. 'After my parents died, I went to live with a great aunt. She wasn't wealthy, for the same reasons as my parents, but I earned a partial scholarship, and she was able to cover the rest.' She lifted a hand tentatively, wondering if Bahira would allow her to pat his nose, and as she did so, Tariq's hands tightened around the reins, ensuring the stallion would remain still. 'Sadly, there wasn't enough left over for the up-keep of a horse,' she joked. 'Besides, when I learned of Elana's mistreatment at the hands—hooves—of one of these animals, I must say, I swore off the idea for life.'

'Is that so?'

She nodded. 'I can't say I've ever regretted that decision.'

'Are you still afraid, Eloise?'

Her lips parted at the direct challenge. He was manipulating her. She understood that, and yet she couldn't quite stop herself from taking the bait. 'I still have a desire to live,' she said, stepping back.

'Do you trust me?'

Something stuck in her throat. She lifted a hand, pulling her hair back from her face. She stared at him, her heart galloping faster than any speed this steed could ever accomplish. 'I don't trust anyone.'

'Do you trust *me*?'

The distinction was like the throwing down of a gauntlet. They both heard it. 'Why?'

His eyes narrowed. 'That's not an answer.'

'What do you want me to say?' she muttered. 'I'm not riding any stupid horse.'

'What about this beautiful, lovely horse?' he asked with a lift of his brow, so her heart turned over in her chest and her eyes jerked to his face.

'He's enormous,' she said with a shake of her head. 'And while he seems perfectly content with you on his back, I don't think the same could be said for me.'

'I didn't say you'd be riding alone.'

She sucked in a sharp breath, shaking her head. 'I can't ride your horse with you.'

'Why not?'

'Come on, don't be so obtuse.'

'It's a horse ride. I'm not asking you to make love to me in the shade of the orange trees.'

Her gut twisted at the immediate, evocative imagery.

'There is something I have learned about fears,' he murmured, stepping off the horse in one swift, easy motion, coming to stand closer to her. 'The feeling of overcoming them is like nothing else.'

She stared up at him, his powerful, confident face, and something shifted inside of her. Did she trust him? Yes. And did she trust herself? She wasn't sure. Only, she knew one thing for sure—while this man would marry her best friend, they had these few days. Days she could spend time with him, be near to him, without crossing any lines of propriety again, but could stockpile memories of the ways he made her feel, something to nourish her in future years.

Elana had sworn off a love match. She didn't want to care about her future husband, it wasn't as though Eloise would be getting close to a man Elana hoped to fall madly in love for. In fact, if Elana was here, she'd be the first one to tell Eloise to let herself go, just a little.

If she turned him down now, she'd always regret it. She knew that.

Torn between loyalty for Elana and a desperate, heartbreaking need to take this one small pleasure, just for herself, she could only stare at him.

'I promise, nothing bad will come of this.'

She let out a shuddering laugh. 'It's not just the horse.'

'Nothing will happen between us.' He was close enough that his breath fanned her forehead and her body lifted in goosebumps. 'You have my word.'

It had to be enough. 'Okay.' Her voice was throaty, the two syllables a commitment to something that terrified and excited her in equal measure. 'But...erm...how exactly do I...?' She gestured to the horse. Where Tariq had made it look easy to dismount from the beast's back, she had no idea how to climb up. She noted there was no saddle nor stirrups.

'May I?'

She tilted her face to his, seeing the way he was looking at her, gesturing to her waist.

She had his word that nothing would happen between them. She had to trust that. She jerked her head in agreement.

She'd *agreed*, but she wasn't *prepared* for the feeling of his hands—broad, strong, capable and confident—wrapping around her sides, holding her steady, lifting her easily, as though she weighed nothing, onto the back of the magnificent beast. And there was no other way to describe the horse, who stood strong and steady as she was placed at the base of his neck. Her hands instinctively sought his neck, patting him, and a moment later, the powerful frame of Sheikh Tariq was at her back, his arms wrapped around her to secure the reins, his face so close to the back of her head that when he spoke it was as though the words were caressing her.

'Are you ready?'

No. She was terrified, as though she were stepping into the fires of hell. How much she wanted him made her want to throw all caution to the wind, to turn around and kiss him, to plunder his mouth as he had hers, to allow her body to answer the siren call of longing that had overtaken her almost from the first moment they'd met. But Elana was at the forefront of her mind, and what she owed her friend, and so she nodded curtly, keeping her gaze focused on the horizon.

'Then let's go.' He kicked the horse's side and the beast responded immediately. There was no opportunity to speak then. Though the horse moved more slowly than he had earlier, when only Tariq was on his back, it was still fast, the hooves cutting over grass first and then, the open field beyond the structured gardens of the palace. It took several minutes before Eloise properly exhaled. She wasn't afraid. She was exhilarated, but she was also intimately aware of every single movement Tariq made, even the subtle way he pulled on the reins to control his horse, or the way his legs moved at her sides, and the way his chest was at her back, framing her, keeping her safe. Protecting her.

She'd never been protected by a single soul in her life. Even her parents hadn't taken care of her. It was impossible not to feel a little in awe of this man, and the way he held her close, ensuring no harm would befall her.

Impossible not to feel a little addicted to that, even when she accepted this couldn't last.

Before she knew it, the grass gave way to sand, crisp and white and she imagined warm underfoot from the full day's sunshine, but the horse rode on, faster now, as if he had a destination in mind and wanted to get there as quickly as possible.

She shivered and perhaps Tariq felt it, or mistook it for fear, because one hand left the reins to clamp around her middle, pinning her back against him, offering extra protection and safety. Only it wasn't safer. Being held by him like this only made her aware of him in a far more visceral way, bringing memories back to mind of the way they'd kissed, of how good it had felt to be held by him.

She bit down on her lip, focusing straight ahead, trying to keep her brain occupied rather than allowing it to slide into a full-blown reflection of that kiss. That mistake.

The desert sands stretched so far ahead that she wondered when the horse was going to turn around. She couldn't say how long they rode in one direction before a rocky outcrop loomed in front of them. It was very nearly night now, the stars brighter overhead, the sky a translucent grey, and the rocks were imposing and unmistakable. When the horse slowed, her ears adjusted to the lack of noise, only to recognise another sound. Running water.

'Where are we?'

He released his grip on her stomach and jumped off the horse, before reaching up and lifting her down. 'I used to come here often as a child.'

'On your own?'

'Not at first,' he said, eyes shifting to hers. 'My father would bring me.' There was another heavy silence, and she knew there was something he wasn't telling her, something he was weighing in his mind, and so she stayed quiet, curious, but determined not to push him.

'As a young boy, I had night terrors. Vivid, terrifying dreams that would wake me in a cold sweat. I'd scream until my lungs burned. Coming here was the only thing that could calm me.'

She looked up at him, surprised. 'I can't imagine you being afraid of anything.'

'Everyone has fears,' he said, gesturing to the rocks in front of them. She recalled what he'd said, just minutes earlier. *There is something I have learned about fears. The feeling of overcoming them is like nothing else.*

She glanced to the horse. 'Do you need to tether him?'

'He will wait for me here.'

'So confident?'

He lifted his shoulders. 'Of course.'

'Because we're quite far away from the palace, Your Highness. If he bolts, I don't particularly want to stay here all night.'

'It is actually a very pleasant place to sleep.'

'You camp here too?'

'On occasion.'

It only cemented the impression she had of this man: that he was so thoroughly of this land, born of it, destined to rule it. 'How does that work?'

His expression showed bemusement. 'There's a swag on the ground...'

She rolled her eyes in an exaggerated gesture of impatience. 'I mean, how do you leave the palace without guards?'

He arched a brow.

'Elana has security with her, always.'

He nodded thoughtfully. 'As she would here.'

'But you don't,' Eloise pointed out.

'I expect our ability to defend ourselves is not equal.'

'You think she's weak?'

'No. More vulnerable to attack though. Besides, as my wife, it would be my duty to ensure her safety—that's a task I take seriously.'

She ignored the *frisson* that ran the length of her spine. 'And you don't need protection?'

He pulled a face and she laughed because it was so absurd.

'I came to an arrangement with the chief of palace security many years ago.'

'Which is?'

'That I inform them of my location. If I'm going to come out here to camp, I bring this.' He lifted a small beacon from his pocket. 'If I press the button, security scrambles to come to me. When I leave the country, it is always with protection. That's our compromise.'

She pulled her lips to the side.

'You don't approve?'

'I don't know, Your Highness. But I can't imagine how unpleasant it would be to have a constant shadow.'

'Does your friend complain?'

Eloise's smile was wistful. 'Elana? Never. She is the most forbearing and sweetest person you'll ever meet. I don't think complaining is in her repertoire.'

Tariq's eyes bore into hers for so long that Eloise jerked her eyes away, looking up at the sparkling constellations overhead instead. 'It must be so peaceful here,' she observed wistfully.

'Don't tell me—you've never slept under the stars before either?'

She shook her head. 'Just on school camps, and that was in dormitories. Not tents.'

'No tents here either. This is all the roof I need.' He gestured to the sky.

It was a magical, romantic notion, and it buried itself deep under her skin, letting her imagine, dream, wonder about this wild, free side of his life.

'What were your nightmares about?'

He tilted his face to hers, scanning her features, and she looked away, not wanting him to see the temptation that must be written there so clearly.

'Nothing discernible,' he said after a pause, so she didn't know if he was gathering his thoughts or keeping something from her. 'It was more an impression than anything firm.'

'An impression of what?'

'Drowning or being burned alive. And not being able to save myself.'

She shivered. 'That's awful.'

He dipped his head in silent agreement. 'Do you still…' She wasn't sure why, but she left the rest of the question unspoken.

'From time to time. Not often now.'

'Are they…' She searched for the right words. 'The result of a specific trauma?'

She could sense him pulling away, closing down the line of questioning, so it was no surprise when he lifted a hand and gestured to something. 'Look.'

With a small sigh of frustration—because she wanted to learn more about him—she followed the direction of his finger and startled. Something was glowing just a hundred or so metres from them. As fluorescent as any light she'd ever seen, but the most striking turquoise colour. 'What is it?' she asked, spellbound.

'A form of algae,' he said softly.

She wrinkled her nose. 'Well, now, I've always thought algae was a little bit gross.'

He laughed, a deep, gruff sound that made her pulse fire.

'It's stunning.'

They moved towards the water's edge.

'Some algal blooms are harmful, even toxic, but this is a natural reaction that takes place here every year. It lasts around a month.'

'I can't believe it's real. It looks like something out of a fairy tale.'

'It's remarkable,' he agreed.

'Everything about this country feels somewhat magical.' She regretted the admission as soon as she'd made it, but it earned Tariq's full attention.

'Oh? What else have you seen that you find magical, little one?'

Little one. The words punctured something dangerously close to her heart. She tilted her chin in defiance, silently reminding herself, and hopefully him, of all the reasons they couldn't give into the temptation that swirled around them.

'The palace. The gardens. The weather. The smell of flowers in the air. The birds.' Right on cue, a night bird made a whipping sound, so light and ethereal the stars almost seemed to titter in response. 'You're very lucky to have grown up here.'

Silence met the pronouncement.

'You don't agree?' she prompted after a moment.

'I love this country,' he said.

She frowned, wondering at the strange distinction. She didn't like secrets at the best of times but feeling that this man was keeping something from her weighed heavily on her mind. And why should it? Because he wanted to marry her best friend? Or because she felt as if something had formed between them that demanded total honesty and transparency?

'There is so much more for you to see,' he said, voice distracted.

She drew her gaze back to his face.

'The palace is one thing, and yes, I agree, it is beautiful, but there is much, much more.'

'And one day, I'll enjoy experiencing that,' she said, somewhat wistfully. 'If the marriage goes ahead.'

The air between them crackled.

'Does that mean you've decided to recommend the match?' His voice held a low, assessing quality.

'Perhaps it's better if you return to the negotiations with her cabinet,' she said with a tightening in her spine. 'While Elana will listen to me, I must listen to them. Only when all considerations have been met can I offer my own opinion.'

'You think the terms of our financial agreements as important as your friend's happiness as my compatibility with her?'

'My friend is very like you,' she said after a pause. 'While I want her to be happy and adored, she wants only what is best for her country. The pressure of being on the throne is great—she wants to make the right decisions for her people.'

'And the marriage is a powerful bargaining chip,' he said. 'After all, I've approached her, she must know I'm motivated to make this succeed. Therefore, she can leverage my interest to better her country's circumstances.'

She was quiet, but her heart was not. It thumped and flipped and groaned at the painful, necessary conversation.

'But perhaps she has miscalculated,' he said after a beat. 'Or perhaps you have. I know that your economy is almost bankrupt. By every metric, Ras Sarat is in a worsening position. It is not Elana's fault—her advisors have failed her—

but she has to shoulder the weight of that. She knows that, in contrast, Savisia is wealthy, powerful and prosperous. Our marriage would benefit Ras Sarat. Is that what she's thinking?'

Eloise stared at him, lips parted. She shouldn't have been surprised by his summation of matters—he was intelligent and his advisors were thorough. Of course he knew how bad things were in Ras Sarat. But somehow it felt as though the rug was being pulled from under her.

She chose her next words with care. 'You seem to have pieced together Elana's motivations, but what of yours?'

He was silent now, his chest moving with each breath he drew.

'You want children, but surely these could be had by any woman of your acquaintance. Why seek out Elana?'

'She is suitable.'

'Suitable? What does that even mean?'

'Born to this life.'

'Why is that essential? Your mother was not a princess when she married your father.'

His eyes narrowed.

'You're not the only one who's done their research.'

'My mother was not royal, you're right.'

'And yet you feel you have to marry a princess?'

'Are you trying to urge me to reconsider?'

'I—' She floundered, caught off guard by his question. After all, that's exactly what she'd been inadvertently doing.

'Is it because you doubt I can make your friend happy? Or because my marriage to her will make *you* unhappy?'

It was far, far too close to home. She blinked, feeling as though the earth was tipping under her feet. 'Don't be ridiculous. This is nothing to do with me.'

She wasn't sure if he believed her, but he didn't speak for a long time, only looked at her, and in that fragment of time, Eloise felt as if her entire soul was laid bare.

She didn't like the feeling; her eyes flickered away.

'We should go back to the palace.'

'Why?'

'Because it's late.'

'Or is it that you don't want to have this conversation?'

Damn it. Damn him. She crossed her arms, her breath ragged. 'I want my friend to be happy. I want this to be simple. I want...' She stopped there. Too many things were on the tip of her tongue and none of them helpful to admit.

But even without speaking the words, they hummed in the air between them, flashes of need, imagery, memories, like little blades floating through the sky. She flinched as one impaled her, the feeling of his mouth on hers, a memory so clear and real that it could have been happening right then and there.

'You're right,' he said, abruptly. 'We should go back.'

It was like being tumbled off a cliff with no warning. She stared at him a long time, wondering what had changed, why he wasn't standing his ground, but then he turned to move, and she had no choice but to follow him.

They walked to Bahira in silence, and when he lifted her onto the horse's back, she almost sobbed at how desperate she was for his hands to hold her longer, to draw her against him in a proper embrace. He didn't.

Do you trust me?

He was showing his trustworthiness, showing that no matter how much they wanted to act on these feelings, they wouldn't, they couldn't. It was forbidden.

'Hold on, little one,' he murmured into her ear, clamping a hand around her waist. 'We'll fly back.'

And he pushed the horse to ride faster, to eat up the distance between them and the palace, to end this delightful, delicious torment more quickly.

He'd wanted to return them back to the palace as quickly as possible. Once the flame had ignited between them, he'd known it would be only a matter of time before one of them acted on it, and he'd been afraid of being the person to weaken first. He'd been concerned that despite having given her an assurance that he could be trusted, perhaps he couldn't be. That his desires would eclipse every other thought and feeling.

But the rapid race back to the palace did nothing to extinguish the flames. The horse jolted beneath them, throwing her back against him. In order to keep Eloise safe, he held her tight, so that every inch of her body was moulded to his, and his arm around her waist couldn't help but feel the soft underside of her breasts, his fingers splayed wide commanded the entire side of her body. How easy it would have been to let his hand slip between her legs, to pleasure her as they rode, to remind her that there was no escaping the delirium of desire they could share.

How wrong it would be, though.

He needed, more than anything, to get her off this horse and safely back into the palace.

His first instinct—to give her space—had been correct. He couldn't be this close and rely on himself to resist her. Every moment was a form of torture. He needed to be free of her and this. Legendary control be damned; he was starting to wonder if he'd ever truly come face-to-face with temptation before.

Finally, the sand gave way to grass and his horse was back on familiar ground, moving toward the stables without needing to be guided. But before they could approach them, he pulled Bahira to a stop.

Though he was Sheikh, and no one would dare gossip about him, the same could not be said for the very beautiful foreigner in their midst. In order to save her from becoming the centrepiece of harmful chatter, he hopped off the horse, but before he could reach up and catch her, she moved one leg over, clearly intending to jump down herself.

He couldn't make a noise fast enough—she was determined, her face pinched, her eyes flashing to his with that same defiance he'd seen out in the desert and then she was sliding down the side. But she'd miscalculated. His beast was far too high for this, for a person of her stature, to dismount without help. He was easily a foot taller than her and used to riding.

He moved forward—too late to warn her, but not to catch her. She hit the ground and immediately fell sideways. She would have landed with a thud if he hadn't intercepted her body's trajectory, catching her and holding her weight in his arms.

'Let me go,' she said, panic in her words. Panic

he understood, because despite what they'd said, something was exploding out of their hands.

'You should have waited for me,' he snapped, anger stirred by worry. For a moment, he'd seen her falling, seen her head cracking against the rock wall to their side, seen her blood stain the grass, and he'd *felt* a wave of nausea, of fear. It shook him.

'I'm okay,' she said, but the words trembled a little. She wasn't okay. But because of her near-fall, or because of the passion stirring between them?

'Are you?'

The question landed at her feet with a thud. She lifted her gaze to his and something seemed to strangle his torso.

This couldn't happen. He couldn't give in to this.

He conjured every iota of decency he possessed, focusing on the reasons he needed to marry Elana, the importance of that union, on the fact that Eloise was Elana's best friend, on the indecency of lusting after her, despite the fact he barely knew his intended bride. It was Eloise he had to protect, Eloise who would be put in a difficult position if anything more happened between them.

So why did he stay there, staring down at her, eyes locked as if he dared not look away?

'I'm glad you showed me that,' she said softly. 'Elana will love to see it for herself one day.'

The reference to Elana sparked anger in his gut. Honour be damned—he wanted to kiss the idea of anyone else from Eloise's mouth. He wanted to lift them up, far away from the palace, from this life, from his duties and needs as a monarch and place them in some tiny corner of the world where he was a man and she a woman, free to explore this hypnotic need.

It was just desire.

Strong, overpowering desire, but a physical need, nothing more. They could explore it, release the urgency and temptation, and then go on with their normal lives. Maybe that's what they both needed, in order to be able to function?

But for Eloise, how could that work? How could she return to Ras Sarat and counsel her friend to this marriage, knowing that she'd slept with him?

And what would it be like for Tariq? He didn't think he'd still be pining over Eloise in a year's time, but he intended to give himself fully to this marriage. How would that work if Eloise was there, in the background, advising Elana? How could it work if he'd slept with his wife's best friend? While both he and Elana seemed in agreement on the practical nature of their marriage, it would still be a legally binding partnership, and he would never allow himself to cheat on her. Eloise would be out of reach forever.

There were myriad reasons to run as fast as the blazes from this, but all he could think about was the beating of a drum, drawing him to her with urgency and all-consuming passion.

Which meant he needed to put as much space between them as humanly possible, and immediately. 'Go inside, Eloise. For God's sake, go now.'

The sound of a small sob pierced something vital in his chest, but then she turned and ran, all the way back to the palace, out of his line of sight but not, regrettably, from his mind.

CHAPTER SIX

IT WAS SOME time later that night, when he should have been fast asleep, that he found an idea spinning around and around until it took a shape he couldn't shake. An idea he should have known better than to indulge, that somehow went from preposterous and wrong to plausible and possible to finally, imperative.

He would take Eloise to see Ala Shathi. The city in the east was, to borrow her word, magical, but it was the mountains surrounding it he more particularly wanted her to see. Mountains that flowed with pristine water were covered with vegetation that offered privacy and seclusion and had long been a port in the storm for Tariq. Even before the business with his father, and the truth of his birth, he'd been drawn to the wildness of Ala Shathi. It was there that he felt most like a man, most unshackled from his royal duties and obligations, from the sense that he carried upon his shoulders the expectations of a country.

Where better to take this woman who couldn't fit into his world in any way, who he couldn't get from his mind?

It was not to seduce her, but to show her the beauty of the east, and to be alone with her, without the fear of being seen, judged, of things being complicated by outside appearances.

He simply wanted to be alone with her. Just for a while. Not to touch her, just to speak to her. To listen to her. To unravel more of what made her tick, to understand her, to lose himself in her.

It was a fantasy; she was forbidden, and he wouldn't forget that. But just for a night or two, he wanted to be selfish. After that, he'd resume his life. He'd get back on track, focusing on the marriage first, and then the business of begetting an heir.

His lips pulled downward grimly. He couldn't turn his mind to that yet. It was across a ravine, with no bridge in sight. He would swim there, or claw his way there, because it was essential to his country and his father's legacy, but he wasn't quite ready yet.

There was something he had to get out of his system first.

'I'm sorry. What did you say?'

'His Highness has the itinerary planned.' The woman spoke more slowly, as though Eloise might be hard of hearing. 'Please, come with me.'

'But where did you say we were going?'

'To tour the eastern provinces.'

'But, why?'

The servant's smile was cool. 'I'm not aware, madam. Would you come this way, please?'

Arguing was clearly pointless. She'd simply have to ask Tariq when she saw him.

She grabbed her handbag on the way out of her suite, keeping pace with the staffer. They emerged onto a driveway about five minutes later and a light breeze rustled past, so Eloise caught at her skirts right as Tariq stepped out of a black four-wheel drive with darkly tinted windows.

Something about it made her mouth dry.

Like his horse, Bahira, it was a car that was so perfectly suited to him. Powerful, enigmatic, thrilling.

'Your Highness,' she murmured, desperate to put them on a more formal footing.

His eyes flashed to hers though and a distillation of memories made her cheeks flush warm.

'Miss Ashworth.' Something twisted in her belly. 'This way, please.' He gestured to the car, at the same time a man in a military uniform opened the back passenger door, making her want to form a joke about being off to execution. Only the intensity of Tariq's expression stalled another word from leaving her mouth.

She stepped up into the seat, aware of Tariq's eyes on her the whole time, so she was reminded of the way he'd helped her on and off the horse the night before and her pulse quickened.

She clipped her seatbelt in place quickly, mind zipping, and when he slid into the backseat beside her, the air in the car zapped with awareness.

Two men took the front seats: a driver and, going by the size and build of the second, a security guard.

Eloise told herself she was glad for the company, glad they weren't alone, but a moment later, Tariq pressed a button and a screen came up, separating them from the front of the car.

She did her best to assume an air of businesslike authority. 'Where are we going, Your Highness?'

'Weren't you informed?'

'Just that we were going "to the east".' She waved a hand in the air, panic threatening to creep into her voice.

His eyes narrowed speculatively. 'It's a beautiful part of the country. I thought you'd like to see it.'

'Tariq,' she murmured, as the engine of the car throbbed beneath them. 'This is—'

He tilted his face to hers, skimming her features with an expression she couldn't read.

'Relax. I have a meeting out that way and thought you would enjoy accompanying me. It's a beautiful part of the country, you'll enjoy it. Plus, you can get to know me some more. It's why you came to Savisia, is it not?'

It all sounded so logical. And yet… 'It's not that simple. Surely you can see that?'

'Why?'

'Because there's danger here,' she said with hushed urgency.

His lips pressed together, but at least he didn't downplay her assessment. 'I see risk, not danger, and risk we can guard against. We both know nothing more can happen between us, and so it won't.'

Eloise could only wish she shared his confidence.

'Hold on a second. What are we doing here?'

He tilted a glance at her. 'What do you mean?'

She pointed a finger towards his Gulf Stream jet. 'Exactly how far are we going?'

A flicker of amusement warred with frustration and impatience. Not with Eloise, so much as with an indefinable force. 'To the east, I told you.'

'But, I mean, that could be an hour's drive away.'

'More like a two-hour flight.'

The colour drained from her skin.

'Relax,' he muttered, his ego smarting from her clear panic. 'I've promised you nothing will happen. I'm not dragging you across the country to have my way with you.'

That jolted her eyes to his and the look in

them had something new shimmering in his gut. Shame. Confusion. He stared back, careful not to reveal a thing.

'I know that.' She held his gaze a moment then turned away, eyeing the plane once more with obvious trepidation. Was she that terrified of being alone with him? Did she trust him so little? 'Then let's go.'

Every step she took was accompanied by a frantic voice in her mind, telling her to confess the truth to him.

Tell him about your fear of flying. That you haven't been on a plane in forever and you don't intend to start now. Tell him you can't bear the thought of being in that tin can, high up above the earth.

But she was embarrassed by her childish phobia and how much it revealed about her, embarrassed to admit such a vulnerability to him, and so she ground her teeth together and took the stairs with a sense of purpose, telling herself all the things the therapist had drummed into her, years ago.

Planes fly every day. They're meticulously maintained. Driving is far more dangerous than flying. That the lack of control she'd felt growing up with two parents who fought so constantly had translated into an anxiety in any circumstance where Eloise wasn't in control, and flying was a perfect example of that. It was too much of a leap of faith, and Eloise didn't trust anyone except Elana.

She was shaking as she stepped onto the plane, but Tariq occupied himself, talking first to the pilot and then taking a call, so Eloise found her own seat and snuggled into it, closing her eyes as if she could blot out her location if she tried hard enough.

The door closed with a bang and she startled, eyes immediately landing on Tariq, who wasn't looking at her. Good. She still didn't want him to know what a chicken she was. It usually helped people overcome their anxiety when they understood the root cause of it, but for Eloise, that hadn't been the case. She dreaded relinquishing control, and there was nothing that would ever make her feel better about that.

The engine began to rumble and she dug her fingers into the armrests as the sound built and built to a deafening crescendo. She focused on the action outside the window, the men in military uniforms moving away from the aircraft, the airport in the distance, loaded with other planes. The emptiness of the skies—clearly a wide berth had been given to the Sheikh's aircraft.

She was so overwrought she barely noticed the extravagant luxury of the plane. She couldn't take in the details, like the plush leather seats, crystal chandeliers, cinema-sized screen at the back of the plane, oak dining table. Any other time, she might have been overwhelmed by the details, but she couldn't notice anything beyond her paralysing fear.

Her heart was firmly lodged in her throat.

She needed to get off the plane.

She flicked another glance to Tariq. He was off the call now, his eyes focused on the view beyond his window, a frown on his face. He was so handsome. Her gut twisted for a whole other reason now, making her blood spin and bubble.

How on earth could she navigate this?

If he married Elana—and he would, he must—then Eloise would have to take a step back. From her best friend. From her life. There was no way she could continue to live as sisters with Elana, while her best friend made a life with herself as Tariq's wife. She loved Elana and wanted only the best for her, but it would be painful beyond bearing to sit on the sidelines and watch that. Eloise would have to leave Ras Sarat, Savisia, the whole area.

She would be cast adrift, again.

Alone.

Friendless.

A lump formed in her throat and she blinked away, right before Tariq turned and looked at her.

She couldn't possibly continue to be near him. It was hard enough now, knowing that the chemistry they felt was technically a mistake. But if he was married to Elana, it would be strictly forbidden, and neither of them could ever betray Elana. Seeing him every day would be a torment.

And not seeing him?

She dipped her head forward, almost glad for the resurgence of her fear as the plane lifted and wobbled a little from side to side as the air currents buffeted the beast of a thing. She made a soft gasping noise, but kept her head down as panic filled her mouth with the taste of metal and she gripped the armrests so hard her fingernails stung.

Two hours?

It wasn't long. She could do it. She had to.

Something was wrong. He'd heard her exclamation shortly after take-off, but then she'd kept doing whatever she was doing, and he'd presumed it was a reaction to something she was reading or watching.

But now, as the jet passed through some mild turbulence, Eloise looked as though she were about to pass out. Her skin had lost all colour, her eyes were huge in her face and her lips were smacking together like she was trying to speak but couldn't.

He stood abruptly and crossed to her, ignoring the now familiar lurching in his gut as he drew near. He crouched down at her side, his pants straining over his haunches as he studied her more closely.

She turned to face him, almost catatonic; she was unrecognisable. He swore. 'What the hell is it?'

She was trembling all over, her hands the worst of all.

'I'm—' But she couldn't speak. Her lips opened and closed without issuing any further noise.

The plane made another little jump and she screamed, pressed a hand to her mouth, then turned away from him, hiding herself. But he'd seen enough; he understood.

She'd driven to Savisia, rather than flying, and at the first sign of the jet, she'd balked. He'd thought it was because it meant being alone with him, but what if it had to do with something more basic, like a fear of flying?

It was the only thing that made sense.

'It's okay,' he murmured, moving past her to the seat opposite, at the window, lifting the armrest between them so he could draw her against his chest. 'It's okay,' he said again, quietly, the words rumbling between them. It didn't help. She was shaking uncontrollably.

He began to worry.

'You're afraid,' he said, needing to know that his suspicions were correct, to rule out anything more sinister.

He felt her sharp nod against him.

'Okay.' Relief washed over him. A fear of flying was something he could manage. He stroked her arm softly, gently, rhythmically, holding her tight, offering security in his grip, and wishing that his altruistic gesture of comfort wasn't making him far too aware of her soft curves and femininity.

'This plane is very safe,' he said. 'The turbulence is normal as we cross the mountains. You will be fine, little one. I promise you.'

Her teeth chattered together. 'How d-do you know?'

'Because I fly all the time.'

'But this time—'

'Will also be safe.'

The trembling didn't subside. All he could do was hold her, and so he did. He held her tight through the turbulence but even once it subsided, he kept her clasped to his chest. At some point, it stopped being because she needed it, and started being because he wanted her there, because he liked feeling her against him, because her breath was warm and her body soft, because his fingers liked trailing over her arms, because she fit so perfectly right where she was. He held her tight and refused to think about how he was breaking the promise he'd made.

He was crossing an invisible line every moment he kept her pressed to him. He knew it, she knew it, yet neither of them did a thing about it.

It was a stolen moment of illicit pleasure, innocent but still wrong.

He didn't fight it.

Something had shifted inside of Eloise. On the flight, she'd been breaking apart, and he'd held her together. They'd shared something, and for Eloise, it had been meaningful. It had also forced her to stop pretending.

There was a force at work between them, something she couldn't keep fighting. It was inconvenient and wrong, and she knew she couldn't act on it how she wanted to, but wasn't she entitled to experience these feelings, just a little? It wasn't a betrayal of Elana to spend time with Tariq, was it? To talk to him and share things with him, to explain a little about her life, including her phobia of flying?

After all, Elana had sent her here to get to know the man. Wasn't that what she was doing?

The city passed in a blur, ancient buildings mingling with modern high-rises, designer shops showing the affluence of the area, giving way to wide boulevards lined with restaurants. Another time, she'd have liked to stop and enjoy it more fully, to immerse herself in the area and discover little laneways and avenues all on her own.

'Do you come out here often?' she asked, turning to face him in the back of yet another limousine, this one accompanied on either side by shiny black motorbikes. He'd served as her protector during the flight. The way he'd held her so tightly, pushing fear from her body, had made it impossible not to be grateful, not to appreciate his size and strength anew.

'Every couple of weeks.'

She lifted her brows. 'But you're based in the capital.'

'I learned as a young boy the importance of remaining visible and informed of each province. In the past, there have been sheikhs who were deemed to be out of touch. I do not want this to be said of me.'

'You are hero-worshipped by your people.'

His eyes found hers and she blushed to the roots of her hair.

'I am fortunately respected,' he agreed after a slight pause.

'As your father was.'

He dipped his head. 'He was an excellent ruler.'

'You've known all your life that this would

be your responsibility one day. Have you always welcomed that?'

There was a hesitation in his features, a look of consternation she didn't understand and then his trademark arrogance was back. 'I was raised for it.'

She frowned. It wasn't quite an answer. She tried again. 'Was there ever a time when you found yourself wishing you had a sibling? Someone who could share the burden with you?'

'My parents couldn't have other children. They tried,' he said, looking towards his window a moment. His Adam's apple bobbed, though, and she knew he was grappling with the confession. She could understand why.

'They tried for years before conceiving me, and then,' he hesitated a moment, 'my mother kept me out of the public eye for the first couple of years of my life. She told me, as a boy, that she hadn't wanted to tempt fate.'

'That's a very natural way to feel,' Eloise sympathised.

'My father was not the heir to the throne and his life then was simply not of much interest to the media or people of Savisia. He lived, more or less, freely.'

She considered that. Much was revealed by his description of his parents' lives. 'And then the Sheikh died in that fire?'

'Yes. My uncle and his wife died before they could have children and the throne passed to my father overnight. We returned to Savisia at once.'

'And ever since, you've known this would be your life.'

'Yes.'

'Did it change things for your father?'

His smile was laced with nostalgia. 'Of course. We went from living as a family to being royal, to having servants and an enormous palace. I could no longer attend school, but rather had long lessons with tutors. I hated being indoors so much. While I enjoyed learning, I always wished to be running, or climbing trees—'

'Or riding a horse,' she posited.

His eyes bore into hers. 'Exactly. Or sleeping under the stars.'

'You must have found a balance at some point in your childhood? After all, it sounds like you were given a fair amount of freedom.'

'I suppose. My father, perhaps because he never thought he would become Sheikh, was determined for me to enjoy a relatively normal childhood. It had to be balanced with the responsibilities and duties of ruling, but I know I enjoyed more freedom than my uncle did, for example.'

'And your children?' she asked quietly, aware that the pain in the centre of her chest was motivated by the knowledge that his children would be of Elana's body. That Eloise would watch her best friend grow round with his seed, would watch Tariq fall in love with a baby he shared with Elana. She tried to ignore the ice-cold tendrils spreading through her veins, and the sense of disloyalty that made Eloise despise herself. 'How will you raise them?'

'I haven't considered it.'

'The main reason for getting married is to beget an heir, yes?'

'Yes.' His hands tightened into fists in his lap before relaxing again.

'So you must have put some thought into this.'

'Why?'

She frowned. 'Isn't it obvious?'

'I presume my wife will want some say in how our children are raised.'

'And if she says they must be sent away to boarding school almost as soon as they can walk?'

'Is that likely?'

Despite the ache in the centre of her chest, she smiled, a sweetly nostalgic smile. 'No. Ellie will be a wonderful and hands-on mother.'

'You've discussed this with her?'

Eloise nodded softly. 'Many times. She's always known she wanted to be a mother. Her own life—' She stopped abruptly, aware that she was speaking about her best friend, perhaps revealing things she would prefer to be kept secret.

'Go on,' he urged.

She searched for how to explain what she meant without revealing more of her friend's innermost thoughts. 'We're very similar,' she said eventually. 'Neither of us grew up with a brother or sister—I think it's why we're so close, that we both recognised that absence, and moved to fill it—and from almost as soon as I've known her, she's spoken openly of her desire to have children. I suppose it was always going to be an expectation on her. To marry, have children, to secure the lineage of her kingdom. When she got engaged before, there was such a sense of relief—for everyone. And then, he died, and it took Elana a long time to...' Her voice trailed off, and she took a breath, searching for the right words. 'She took it very hard. She loved him, a lot, and just learning to put one foot in front of the other again took months. It was at least a year before I saw her laugh again. And all the while, her government has been pressuring her to move on, to marry quickly, to have children. The idea of which has been, until recently, anathema to her.'

'But now?'

Eloise gnawed on her lower lip, then stopped when his eyes fell to the gesture, his own expression far too fascinated to be able to ignore. She straightened her spine and stared beyond him, to the palace they were approaching.

'Time has passed. It's helped. She's ready.'

He hesitated a moment. 'I'm glad. This marriage makes sense. For both of us.' His voice was dark though, the words tinged with heaviness.

The car turned towards two dark black, wrought-iron gates. They were heavily guarded. She watched as a soldier approached the car and then bowed low towards the darkly tinted windows.

'And what about you, little one?'

She startled at the use of the term, somehow so intimate and personal, here, on the footsteps of his grandiose royal home.

'What about me?' Her voice was thick, hoarse.

'Do you intend to marry and have children? To live happily ever after?'

'I think,' she said on a rushed breath. 'That "happily ever after" can take many shapes.'

'Yours doesn't include children of your own?'

She toyed with her fingers in her lap. 'I don't think so.'

'Why not?'

Up until a few days ago, she would have given her standard answer: that she liked being on her own. Inwardly, she would have admitted that she hated the idea of being part of a family, given what her experience of family was like. Seeing the way her father was with her mother had given her a unique prism through which to view promises of love. She was naturally suspicious of the whole idea. But then she'd met Tariq and a different kind of resistance had stitched its way into her soul. How could she ever think of marrying and having children with anyone else?

It terrified her to realise how completely he'd taken over her soul in such a short period of time. When had that happened? And why hadn't she stopped it? Because she couldn't? Because she hadn't realised it was happening until it was too late? It was immaterial. The damage was done and she'd have to live with the consequences.

'Eloise?'

She flinched a little, then forced a tight smile. 'It doesn't matter, does it?'

Because that was true. They needed to remember why she was there, and it certainly wasn't to discuss her own future plans. They were, in any event, in such disarray, she couldn't have elaborated on them for a million pounds.

'For some reason, it does. Humour me.'

The car drew to a halt but Tariq put down his window and, with a single hand gesture, stopped the four armed men from approaching the car. His place within the kingdom was formidable, but it wasn't simply a birthright. This man had a power that came from within, a way of speaking and being that spoke of true authority with every part of him.

'I've never been able to picture myself playing happy families.'

'Because your family was so far from that?'

Her eyes widened at his perceptive comment. Ordinarily, she might have obfuscated but with Tariq, a need to be completely honest drove through her. She nodded quickly, not meeting his eyes.

'Was he physical with her?'

She didn't look at him but nodded again.

His breath hissed from between his teeth.

'She was just as bad,' she muttered. 'It was an incredibly volatile relationship, swinging from over-the-top love one moment to deep, vitriolic rage and hatred the next. Some people might have, romantically, described it as "passionate", but it wasn't. It was madness. Utter, overpowering, lunatic behaviour. They should have ended it years earlier, but they were too addicted—to each other and the drama. Watching it from the sideline was hard enough, but then, more often than not, I was right in the middle of it.'

He reached out, pressing a finger to her chin, lifting her face to his, and the compassion she saw in his eyes made her want to weep.

'Please, don't look at me like that,' she asked, trying to rally her features into a mask of courage.

'How am I looking at you?'

'Like I might fall apart if you let go.'

His eyes shuttered closed for a few moments, his lips parting as he inhaled. 'That's not what I think.'

'No?'

'I think you are strong,' he said quietly, moving closer by degrees, so their mouths were only an inch apart. 'I think your life has made you strong, as mine has me. I think we share a lot, Eloise.'

It wasn't a declaration of love, and she couldn't have accepted that anyway, but his words sent her heart soaring into the stratosphere, and the smile that lifted the corner of her lips was genuine and immediate. She hated herself for feeling this way around him, but she couldn't stop it. All she could do was hold herself back from acting on it, and that she intended to do with every last fibre of her body.

She pulled away from him until her back was against the seat and her eyes were on the building beyond them, and when she could trust herself to speak, she said, 'What is this place?'

She wasn't sure if his rough expulsion of breath denoted frustration or something else, but she didn't look at him, and when he spoke, his voice was bland, all the emotion carefully flattened out of it. 'One of my palaces. My favourite, in fact. It's where I thought my family might live.'

That pulled at her. She whipped her face to his, lips parted. He'd brought her here to assess it for Elana. It was a relief, on some level, but also, a pain.

'When I finished school, I joined the army. I was stationed out of the city here. They were some of the best years of my life; I have an affinity with the east.'

A thousand questions blew through her. 'I remember reading that you'd served in the army,' she said quietly. It was one of the many things his people adored about him—his genuine love of service.

His lips flattened a little. With disapproval? 'I wish that you did not know so much about me.'

Her eyes widened. 'I didn't research you for the fun of it. My job demanded that I come to Savisia prepared.'

'I know. Of course. It's only—' She waited, watching him carefully. 'There are things about me that *I* would like to tell you. Because I like speaking with you, Eloise.'

Her heart trembled. Danger felt imminent. 'You can speak to me,' she said, trying desperately to keep her voice casual. 'That's also part of my job, remember? Now, why don't you show me this palace so I can tell you if Elana will like it.'

CHAPTER SEVEN

THERE WAS NOTHING about the palace *not* to like. While it was grand and beautiful and very old, it was also smaller than the palace in the capital city, and somehow felt more conducive to family living. There were gardens and swimming pools and the view of the city was quite stunning, so she could easily imagine the joy of living in such a home, of taking children out into the ancient city for ice cream and treats, to exploring the markets they'd driven past, with the enormous spice towers. Of course, it wouldn't be her experiencing any of that, but Eloise knew her best friend well enough to know that Elana would love living here as much as Eloise would have.

The day progressed, and Eloise, left to her own devices for much of it, felt a strange tiredness overtaking her. The heat, she imagined. She stifled a yawn and then, when half an hour later there was still no sign of Tariq, asked one of the women who'd been assigned to guide her if there was a sitting room she could use, to have some iced tea and take a break.

She was immediately shown to a delightful parlour with sumptuous furnishings and large windows with golden shutters that showed a view all the way into the city. She sat herself down and inhaled, spice and history filling her soul.

Sometime after enjoying a tray of refreshments, with Tariq still not in evidence, she kicked off her shoes then lifted her feet onto the sofa, and pressed her head to the armrest, intending only to close her eyes for a moment. Except her dreams had been so tormented of late, sleep such a difficult commodity to come by, that she fell into slumber, a dreamless, heavy repose, that lasted until the sun was low in the sky and the night birds began to sing.

Tariq found her fast asleep. He dismissed his servants immediately, stepping into the room and clicking the door shut silently, staring at her from across the room with a growing sense of unease in his gut.

Their situation was precarious and they both knew that.

Asleep like this though, it was easy to fantasise about waking her with a kiss, about pulling back the threads of her dreams with his body. His nostrils flared and he crossed his arms, needing to dismiss those thoughts. Too much was riding on his marriage to Elana to engage these fantasies.

She was just a woman, like any woman he'd met.

That wasn't true and he knew it, even as he

forced the rhetoric down his throat. But she couldn't be more special to him than that. He had to marry Elana of Ras Sarat. He needed her royal bloodline to legitimise his right to rule Savisia. It was a pre-emptive strike against any future claim to the throne. And it was apparent that *any* claim would hold more merit than his own, despite the legal rights adoption conferred on him. Were he an ordinary citizen that would be credible, but belonging to the royal family was different. In a country like Savisia, which prided itself on its royal family's connection to the ancient bloodline of sheikhs, his presence would be an insult. He wasn't even born of Savisian parents! Were there a worthy contender to replace him, he would have relinquished the role he wasn't sure he deserved, but those who might seek power for themselves were hardly the sort who should possess it, and in this case, there was only a distant cousin, a man who was of questionable enough character for Tariq to know that abdicating wasn't the right option for the people of Savisia.

He had to do what was right. He owed his father that much, his mother too, and his people. He would continue to do his duty, to marry a princess, so that his own children would grow up free from this sense of illegitimacy.

Hardening his resolve, ignoring a burning need

for Eloise that was overtaking him, he walked to the sofa and pressed a hand to her shoulder, intending only to wake her.

But she shifted, and his hand slipped, moving from her shoulder to the top of her breast, and he froze. His limb was no longer within his control. His fingers sat there, lightly against her flesh but feeling the gentle swell of her and almost igniting.

She blinked her eyes open, confused at first and then smiling, welcoming him with that look she had, so he ground his teeth, wanting her and knowing he couldn't have her, his body completely at war with his mind.

'Hello, Your Highness,' she murmured, and her voice was so lightly flirtatious, without the heaviness that accompanied them always, as both worked to deny their instincts, that he knew she'd forgotten all the reasons they couldn't act on these feelings. She'd been dreaming, perhaps even dreaming of him.

He was at a crossroads. Honour pulled him in one direction, clearly dictating that he should step back and speak firmly, but desire drew him in another, skittering all of his very best intentions... Curiosity pushed his finger higher, to the pulse point at the base of her neck. He held his fingers there a moment, eyes on hers, watching for a signal, no matter how small, that she didn't want him to touch her.

She blinked languidly and stretched a little. Was she fully awake? Or did she believe this too was a dream?

'How did you sleep?' Her pulse thundered beneath his touch.

'I was tired.' She stretched again and then, as his fingers trailed along her collarbone, towards the lower part of her neck, she startled and sat up, knocking his hand free in the motion, face pale.

He dropped his hand to his side, staring down at her, waiting for her to say something next.

'I didn't mean to sleep,' she said quietly, eyes fixed on the carpet at their feet. 'It's the heat, I think.'

'It's been a long day. My meetings were not as easily concluded as I thought. I hope you weren't bored?'

'Not at all.' They were being so polite; it infuriated him. She moved to stand, carefully keeping at least a metre of space between them. 'I've enjoyed touring the palace. It's beautiful.' She paused, eyes washing over him a moment then landing on the carpet again. 'Elana would love it here.'

He wanted to tell her Elana could go to hell, but the truth was, that wasn't the case. He needed this marriage to the Princess. Besides, he suspected Elana's best friend wouldn't exactly appreciate the sentiment, no matter how much they desired one another.

'Are you ready to leave?'

Her gaze lifted to his again. 'Already?' She squeezed her eyes shut, as if regretting the word.

He understood her sentiment, and an idea he'd already dismissed as ill-conceived latched in his mind, demanding his indulgence. 'Not back to the palace,' he said quietly. 'There's something else I'd like to show you first.'

There was wariness in her features. 'For Elana?'

He dipped his head once, when the truth was, this was his own personal place, somewhere he wanted to show Eloise, because he wanted *her* to see it. This was nothing to do with the Princess he knew he had to marry.

'Okay,' she agreed softly. He fought an urge to reach for her hand and hold her close to his side as he guided her from the room.

'Are you sure you know where you're going?' It was the first either of them had spoken in over an hour. The streets of the city had given way to rural stretches of road and then, finally, to mountains—narrow roads barely illuminated by the dusk light, but sufficiently enough that she could see an increasingly steep drop out of her window, with thick vegetation on his. Tariq drove these roads as though he knew them well, and just the sight of him behind the powerful car, was doing funny things to her pulse. Behind them, another car followed—a four-wheel drive packed with four security guards.

'*They establish a perimeter when I'm in the woods,*' he'd said carelessly, as they'd set off from the palace, and she'd tried to tamp down on the idea of this rugged mountain of a man out in nature.

'Do you seriously doubt me?'

She found herself grinning despite the tension that had been coiling in her belly since that afternoon. 'We seem to be in the middle of nowhere is all.'

'Not quite.'

'Nearly the middle of nowhere?'

'About ten clicks west of it.'

She lifted her brows. 'It will be dark soon.'

'That tends to happen at night.'

Her lips parted. 'Tariq…'

'Relax. We're not staying out here.'

She expelled a shaky breath. It wasn't that she hated the idea…quite the opposite. But she knew they had to get back to reality, sooner rather than later. Even if that meant taking another ride on his private jet.

He continued to drive, navigating the turns

in the road expertly, leaving Eloise free to look over the edge into the ravine below, or to chase the golden orb of the sun as it continued to drop low and finally disappear into the horizon. At some point, the four-wheel drive that had been following them, peeled off, presumably to establish the perimeter he'd mentioned.

'I like privacy,' he explained, as if somehow intuiting her thoughts.

'Where will they be?'

'They set up a checkpoint on this road—the only way to reach the cabin.'

She nodded slowly, her heart in her throat.

When he brought the car to a stop, half an hour later, the sky was still glowing with the last hints of purple and gold, the clouds silver-fringed pewter. She looked around, her gaze landing on a cabin made of stone in the middle of a dense woodlands.

'What is this place?' she murmured, craning forward to see it better.

'Somewhere I like to come when I want to get away.'

She turned in her seat to face him fully. 'This is yours?'

'All this land belongs to the palace,' he said, gesturing to the mountains they were on.

She let out a low whistle. 'And your guards, how close are they?'

His eyes locked to hers for a moment too long and her stomach tightened into knots. 'Close enough.'

'As in...?'

'You don't have to worry, Eloise. I gave you my word I wouldn't touch you, and I won't. I just wanted to show you this place.'

She shivered, but it was not a shiver of fear so much as anticipation. She ignored it, her eyes roaming the cottage with undisguised curiosity. 'Okay.'

'Come on.'

He stepped out of the car and a moment later was at her door, opening it before she could, holding it for her to step out. Her heart skidded into her ribs. 'Thank you,' she murmured, careful to step around him, careful that they didn't touch. It didn't matter though. The air between them seemed filled with electrical pulses, so whether she touched him or not, she was conscious of a zapping just beneath her skin.

He gestured towards the cabin and she walked beside him, several feet away—still getting used to the idea of being completely alone with him. There was a crude path, paved with gravel; he left it for her to walk on. They approached the cabin and he lifted a hand, running it over the stone. 'My father and I built this, many summers ago.'

She was filled with awe. 'Really?'

'He believed we were men first, sheikhs second. The royal life threatens to disconnect one from reality; he wanted to avoid that.'

She echoed his movement, tracing the building with her palm, feeling the roughness of the materials and shivering as she pictured Tariq in the act of constructing it, laying stone by stone until the work was completed. 'You must have been very proud of yourself.'

'There was a great sense of achievement.'

'Why did you choose to build it here?'

'This was one of my father's favourite places, before it was mine.'

'You'd come out here together?'

He nodded once.

'And you still like to escape here, whenever you can,' she murmured, as he went to the door and moved something aside to reveal a pin code. He entered a succession of six digits and the door clicked open.

'Yes.' He stood back to allow her to enter first, then flicked on a light switch. She stepped into the cabin, looking around and smiling, because it was basic but also, absolutely charming. The layout was simple enough: a living area with a kitchen, wooden table and chairs and a single sofa. Two doors came off the space, both were open. One revealed a double bed, the other a bathroom.

'Very rustic,' she said, flicking a quick glance at him.

'It's for camping,' he said with a shrug. 'And hunting.'

'Hunting?'

'A national pastime.'

She shivered.

'Not to your liking?'

'Not particularly,' she said, pulling her lips to the side. 'I've never been a fan of the idea.'

He moved closer almost unconsciously. 'Then you don't have to hunt.'

'I'm glad. I'd hate to think there was some royal decree demanding I take arms against innocent animals.'

'Not on this occasion,' he responded in kind, lightly teasing. Goosebumps lifted over her skin.

It was too easy to flirt with him, to tease him, to joke with him. Too easy to slip into a conversational groove. She had to keep things focused on Elana. That was the reason she was here.

'Her Highness is an avid outdoors person,' she said after a beat, and she knew she wasn't imagining the way his eyes darkened.

'Is she?'

'She's the only reason I was able to survive the school camp experience, in fact.'

'You didn't enjoy it?'

She shook her head quickly.

'You said it was dormitories, though? That's not exactly roughing it.'

She hesitated a moment, the truth something she'd only ever told Elana. And yet, here, with this man, she felt it slipping through her like a river she couldn't dam, no matter how hard she tried. Slowly, she moved towards the kitchen, simply to have something to do with her hands.

'When I was younger, and my parents would fight, my mother would lock me in a closet. Ostensibly, it was to protect me. I don't know, maybe she thought sound couldn't travel through the flimsy walls,' she muttered, so caught up in her admission that she didn't see the way his body had grown tense. 'I hated it. I was scared of the dark. Scared of their fighting. Even more scared of the silence that followed. Sometimes she would forget me—'

He swore, and she looked at him, pain in her eyes.

'I'd be too scared to bang on the walls, in case they got angry with me, so I'd sit there and wait.'

He moved closer and it didn't occur to her to mind.

'I've hated small rooms ever since. Any enclosed spaces, in fact.'

'Airplanes?' he prompted gently.

'I think that's more about a loss of control,' she said with a lift of her shoulders. 'I get...anxious...when I have to rely on others.'

His eyes narrowed perceptively.

'I saw a therapist for a while, but it didn't help. I find I just avoid cramped rooms as much as possible, and I'm okay.'

'How's this?' He gestured to the cabin surrounding them.

'Actually,' she frowned, 'it's not so bad. It's bigger than the camp dorms,' she said with a tight smile.

'I'm glad. I wanted you to see it.'

Her heart tripped over itself. It wasn't the first time he'd said it, but she didn't for one second think he meant he wanted her to see it as Elana's advisor. This was personal. 'Why?'

His expression was hard to read. 'I don't know,' he admitted, finally. 'But it felt important.'

She toyed with her fingers. It felt important to her, too.

'Are you hungry?'

She looked around the kitchen. 'Why? Are you hiding some gourmet snacks in here somewhere?'

'Not quite gourmet.' He grinned. 'But the

freezer should have something, and the stove works.'

It was, oh, so very tempting, but the idea of staying with him for dinner was fraught with possibilities, and danger.

'I think we should go back,' she said, without meeting his eyes.

'Is that what you want?'

Frustration bubbled over inside her chest. Frustration at the way he was pushing her, tempting her, deliberately showing her a place like this that meant so much to him, even when they knew how close they were moving to an invisible line they couldn't step over.

'Damn it, this isn't about what I *want*, Your Highness.'

A muscle clenched at the base of his jaw. 'You need to call me Tariq.'

'You are the Sheikh of Savisia—'

'I'm aware of that.' He crossed his arms over his broad chest and a thousand sparks ignited in her bloodstream. 'But when I am alone with you, I am simply a man.'

She stared at him, angry and frustrated and lost. How could she argue with that? When they were together, that's exactly how it felt to her, too. There was no longer a question of rank between them, they were simply a man and a woman with the kind of chemistry that was rare and unique.

'Tariq,' she said on a soft sigh, lifting a hand and tucking her hair behind her ear. His eyes latched to hers and the world seemed to stop spinning. Everything grew very still, and despite the fact she knew his guards were out there, somewhere, she felt as though they were the last two people on the planet.

'Let's stay here for dinner,' he said gruffly.

Oh, she wanted that. Here, on the edge of the earth, where nothing else seemed to matter. 'We shouldn't.'

His eyes sparked. 'Why not?'

She bit down on her lower lip. 'You know the answer to that.'

'I'm asking you to join me for dinner, not a night in my bed.'

Her cheeks flushed red, heat overwhelming her body as the idea of that sent her senses into overdrive.

'I—' Her heart was in her throat, her breath constricted as she tried to form two coherent thoughts, to put into her words how she felt and what she wanted. In the end, all she could do was nod.

'Good.' His answering nod of approval skittered her nerves further and a moment later, he was stepping into the kitchen, so close to her that Eloise's tummy twisted into a tangle she'd never felt before. He turned his back, giving her an opportunity to relax, and also to regard him. The two were incompatible; she settled on staring.

He moved with a natural athleticism; a lithe strength contained in even the simplest of movements. He pulled a container from the freezer, placing it on the bench, then crouched down to remove a pan from the cupboard. She watched, fascinated, as he opened the Tupperware then emptied it into the pot, placing it on the stove. A moment later, he turned to face her, his expression lightly amused, as though he recognised she'd been staring at him completely unreservedly.

Chastened, she stood straighter, a defensive tilt to her chin.

'Will you be offended if I remove my thobe?'

She furrowed her brow.

'It's easier to cook,' he explained, and when she didn't immediately refuse, he turned his back and carefully undid the button that held it in place, unwrapping it from his body and laying it with care across the back of a chair.

Her mouth went dry. It wasn't as though he'd stripped naked—he wore traditional cuffed trousers and a loose-fitting cotton shirt—but there was something so intimate about him undressing in front of her, even if just down to clothes. She looked away quickly, cheeks heated.

'How old were you when your parents died?'

It was a direct question, asked as if he had a right to the information, and strangely, she didn't resent that.

'Eleven.'

He nodded thoughtfully, moving to the fridge and removing a bottle of mineral water. 'How did it happen?'

Another direct question. She focused on the deft movements of his hands, shucking the lid off the bottle, then pouring it into two thick glasses.

'A car accident.' His hand shifted, slightly, so the top of the bottle knocked a glass. It was a strange, jarring movement from a man who was in such possession of himself. 'They'd been at a party.'

'You weren't with them?' His voice sounded normal, though. Nothing untoward. She frowned, remembering that night with a heavy heart, as always.

'No. They left me home.'

'Alone?'

She lifted her shoulders. 'I liked to be home alone.'

Sympathy softened the corners of his eyes. She blinked away, self-conscious.

'I read a lot,' she elaborated.

'Because it helped you escape?'

'Exactly.' Her heart expanded with how quickly he'd understood. Their eyes met and the world seemed to contract and expand rapidly, so she wondered how everyone didn't feel the gigantic fault lines forming. 'Somewhere in the early hours of the morning, a policeman came to the house. My mother had survived long enough to tell them about me.'

'How did you feel?'

She took a gulp of mineral water. 'My parents had just died. How do you think I felt?'

'Conflicted,' he responded, without missing a beat. Her lips parted in surprise.

It was like he had a direct tunnel into her thoughts.

'I was devastated. I loved my parents very much,' she insisted defensively, cupping the glass with both hands. 'But yes,' she admitted slowly, reluctantly, and yet, also gladly, because she'd never spoken to another soul about this—even Elana. It was impossible to admit without feeling that it made her a terrible person, and yet with Tariq, that didn't seem important.

'For a moment, I was relieved. Their fighting was so awful, Tariq.' Her eyes swept closed. 'So soul-destroying. For a brief moment, when I realised it would stop, that I would no longer have to live with it, I felt…at peace.' She winced. 'I know that's awful.'

He reached over, pressing his hand to hers. It was a gesture of comfort, and it did comfort her.

She felt warm, and complete. 'Life is complicated.' His voice was deep. 'Love even more so.'

'I thought you'd never been in love?' she
prompted, the words catching in her throat.

'Romantic love,' he said with a shrug, not removing his hand from hers. 'But I have parents.
I know that things are not always simple.'

'In what way?'

His features tightened but his eyes were kind.
Her heart was mush. 'Relationship dynamics, expectations. Children have to live with the consequences of their parents' decisions. It's not always
easy.'

'Why do I feel like there's something you're
not telling me?'

His grin was dismissive, but a sixth sense, an
innate understanding of this man, told her he
was hiding something from her. She hated that.
She wanted to peer deep into his soul and see
all of his secret recesses as she knew he could
hers. 'Because I am the Sheikh of Savisia: there
are a great many state secrets I must take to the
grave with me.'

She expelled a soft sigh, letting him get away
with it. 'Is what we're eating one of those things?'

His smile deepened and now her heart skipped
so many beats she wondered if it had stopped
working. 'Be patient; soon, you'll see.'

CHAPTER EIGHT

SHE SLEPT SOUNDLY at his side, so beautifully peaceful that he found his eyes straying to her far more times than was wise, given he was navigating the tight corners of the mountain roads and it was almost pitch black.

He hadn't intended for them to stay at the cabin so long. Hell, he hadn't *intended* for any of it to happen. Bringing her here had been a spur of the moment decision, a desire to share something with her that had made no logical sense. Whatever form his marriage took, he wasn't foreseeing a relationship in which he brought his bride out here. This was *his* space. His bolt hole, and haven.

So why Eloise? Why now?

A loud noise demanded his attention and he immediately pressed his foot to the brake, assessing the situation, all senses on alert. Ears heard the rumble, eyes registered the dust first, plumes silhouetted against the night sky, the falling trees next, and then the smell of clay, finally, the rumble of their car. He swore harshly, loud enough to wake her, so she sat bolt upright.

'What is it?'

'An earthquake,' he said with confidence—

they were not uncommon in this region, though not usually of this magnitude. 'And a landslide.'

A tree fell, right in front of them, blocking their path.

Eloise's breath was loud, but she sat perfectly still, her eyes staring through the windscreen, as though her powers of concentration could somehow supercharge his to ensure their safe departure.

'It's blocked the road. We'll have to go back to the cabin,' he added, without looking at Eloise.

'Oh.' A tiny sound in the void of the car.

He heard it, and he understood.

They'd both been very careful to skirt around their attraction, but the cabin was quicksand. He closed his window, staring straight ahead while waiting for his heart to stop racing so hard.

'It will be all right,' he assured her, and the statement was a blanket reassurance, covering their present state of emergency, as well as the future possibility of carelessness. It was also a promise to himself, one he badly needed.

His fingers tightened on the wheel and he undertook a five-point turn, so he could drive forward and reach the cabin as quickly as was possible.

It looked different now. Ridiculous, given they'd only left here an hour or so earlier. But that had been after a quick bite to eat, polite conversation about the state of politics in the region—a conversation in which she'd been pleased to more than hold her own, to show her knowledge of the various issues facing both Ras Sarat and Savisia. After all, she advised Elana on a plethora of subjects. As the evening had progressed, she'd felt his attention narrowing, his questions growing more specific, as though he was testing her. But to what end?

'Go inside,' he said. 'I will just call my guards and inform them of our situation.'

'Maybe they'll send someone tonight,' she said, hopefully.

'I will make sure they don't,' he responded quickly. 'It would imperil their lives, and I do not subscribe to the ridiculous notion that my life holds more value than any of theirs. First light will have to do.'

She turned back to the cabin, butterflies exploded in her belly.

He stalked to the door and pressed in his code again, pushing the thing open. 'I'll only be a moment.'

She nodded, excitement and anxiety at war within her. Stepping into the cabin, she reached for the light switch, flicked it, then frowned when it didn't do anything. She flicked it again.

'Uh-oh.' She pulled her phone from her

pocket, turning on the torch function, moving into the kitchen and rooting around for candles and matches. She presumed both would be available, given there was a fireplace in the corner. In the third drawer down, she found what she was looking for, and busied herself arranging candlesticks in glasses, bunching them together.

The result, a few minutes later, was more light, but far, far too much ambience. Her veins felt sticky. He stepped into the cabin, and even in the dim light of the candles, she saw the look on his face as he scanned the room.

'The lights aren't working.'

He moved to the switch and tried it himself. Nothing.

'The generator should still be powering things. I'll go and inspect it.'

He departed quickly, evidently as keen to avoid a night in a candlelit cabin with her, as she was him. She paced the floor as she waited, listening to the sound of the night now—birds, the breeze in the trees, and nothing else. It was so quiet up here. So peaceful.

She stopped walking and closed her eyes, inhaling deeply. It was easy to understand why he and his father would come here.

'It's fried,' he said with a shake of his head, striding back into the cabin.

'Fried?'

'A casualty of the earthquake. It will have to wait until tomorrow.'

'Candles it is then,' she said, aiming for a light-hearted tone and failing.

He looked around, and she almost laughed, because for the first time since meeting him, he looked lost.

She understood.

They were fighting this thing so hard, and yet here they were, stranded in a beautiful cabin on the edge of the world, as stripped away from the concerns of royalty and nationhood as it was possible to be. But none of it was real—their isolation was just an illusion. In the morning, he'd still be the Sheikh of Savisia, destined to marry her best friend.

She crossed her arms over her torso and moved to the sofa, weaving around him carefully, sitting right on the edge.

'I'll check the bed,' he said stiffly. She heard the tone of his voice and understood. He was holding on to his control carefully, but it was taking effort.

This was insufferable.

'What for?'

'So you can sleep in it.'

She furrowed her brow. 'You can't be meaning to sleep on this?' she said, her hand slicing through the air. 'It's far too small.'

'I'll sleep on the floor.'

'You'll do no such thing,' she responded with a shake of her head. 'I'll take the sofa; you have the bed.'

'Absolutely not.'

'Why? It's logical.'

'You are a woman and the bed is more comfortable. Naturally you should sleep there.'

She didn't know how to tell him she wouldn't be doing much sleeping, knowing he was within a couple of metres of her. 'That's ridiculously old-fashioned. I'm fine with the sofa.'

'But I'm not.'

'Yeah, well, what are you going to do about it?'

'Need I remind you I'm the Sheikh of Savisia?'

'Believe me, I'm well aware of that.'

The air crackled between them.

'I'm not going to have this argument with you,' he said, all regal hauteur.

'Good. We don't need to argue.' To emphasise her point, she snuggled down on the sofa. It was small enough that her legs were bent up, but she closed her eyes and pretended contentment.

The swishing of his thobes told of his departure, and she celebrated the micro-victory, until a moment later he returned. 'The bed's fine. No spiders. You can go in there now.'

She sat up, staring at him and then she burst out laughing. 'This is ridiculous,' she said with a shake of her head, and then, he was laughing too, hands on his hips, eyes resting on her face. 'I'm not even tired right now.'

'You were asleep in the car.'

'What can I tell you? I guess an earthquake and a landslide shake you right back awake.'

'A fair point.'

She looked around the cabin. 'Do you have anything to do here?'

He lifted a brow. 'Perhaps you should be more specific.'

'A board game? Cards?' she rushed to clarify.

He moved to a small bookshelf and withdrew a silver box, carrying it towards her. He hesitated, gesturing to the other side of the sofa. 'May I?'

Her heart in her throat, she nodded. It was, after all, his cabin.

As soon as he sat down, she felt the error of her decision. They were so close. The sofa wasn't large enough for them to sit side by side without touching. She went to move, to jerk to stand, but his hand on her knee stilled her.

'It's okay,' he said, gruffly. His smile was slow. Gentle. 'It's just cards.'

It didn't feel like 'just cards'. Not then, and not when he began to speak slowly, his accent heavy, recounting the rules of the game his father had taught him—the subtle gathering of houses to form a suite—patiently explaining for the first few hands then setting about ruthlessly demolishing her until she learned enough lessons to hold her own.

It didn't feel like 'just cards' as they laughed in unison at a poor twist of fortune, nor when he commended her for beating him, his eyes glowing with something suspiciously like pride.

It felt like *so much more.*

'I…' The word hung between them. She pulled back a little. 'I should go to bed.'

'You're tired now?'

'Not really,' she responded. 'But I should go to bed anyway.' If she stayed there any longer, she wasn't sure what would happen. His promise that everything would be fine felt as shaky as the earth outside the cabin.

'If you wish.' He stood, his ingrained manners fluttering something in the region of her heart. 'There are spare toothbrushes in the bottom drawer of the bathroom. Soap in the shower. Make yourself at home.'

She nodded without a word. She didn't trust her voice to speak.

There was no hot water so she shunned the idea of a shower, but she brushed her teeth gratefully, then stared at her reflection in the simple mirror above the sink. Slowly, she pulled her hair from its neat chignon, letting it fall down her back. She splashed her face with water then towelled it dry, aware she looked younger without the light make-up she habitually wore. There wasn't much she could do about her clothes—she didn't dare remove a single item—but when she stepped out, it was to find Tariq hadn't shared her reservations. He'd stripped down to his cuffed pants. His torso was bare, the pants slung low on his waist.

The breath exploded from her lungs and she could only stand there and stare at him, everything inside of her burning at fever pitch.

'I've put a spare tunic of mine on the bed, in case you'd prefer to sleep in it.'

Her lips were parted and refused to come back together. Her eyes wouldn't cooperate. They feasted on him even when she knew she needed to look away.

He made no effort to conceal himself, but rather, submitted to her inspection, standing like a very desirable statue. Something tilted inside of her.

'You have to understand,' she said, quickly, even when he hadn't asked. 'That Elana is very special to me. I don't have any family, but I have her, and I would never do anything to hurt her. Ever. I would never betray her.'

He stood very still. 'Am I asking you to?'

Her brow furrowed and then, gradually, her

gaze lifted higher, so their eyes met. 'If I asked you to kiss me, would you?'

His eyes flared and heat simmered between them.

'I can't ask you to. That's my point.'

'I am not engaged to her, you know.'

'But you intend to be.'

He dipped his head. 'Perhaps.'

Her heart raced with a shameful degree of hope and she despised herself for that.

'But that is in the future. We're here, now.'

She shook her head. 'You know that's just a technicality.'

'Then answer me this,' he said quietly. 'If our wedding plans become official, the date will be set some months in the future, at least. Six months, let us say? To allow everyone time to organise the essentials. Do you think I will stay here, celibate and alone for half a year or more?'

She gasped, his words far more hurtful than surely he intended.

'You said you'd be faithful to her.'

'And from the moment I say my vows, I will be. Until then, I consider myself a free agent.'

'Well, I don't,' she muttered. 'And even if I thought that of you, I'm not…not free to do anything with you, I mean. So if you want to "free agent" yourself around town, you just have to get through tonight and then you can go and find someone else to take to bed tomorrow night. Okay?'

'I don't want someone else. I want you.'

The bold statement hung between them. A moment later, he dragged a hand through his hair and she felt her heart lurch crazily.

'I want you.' The words were said with even more determination. 'I wish I didn't. I hate that I do. I have tried to fight it, to control it, to ignore it, but it's here, inside of me.' He pressed a hand to his chest. 'I don't know what you did to me. Some form of voodoo or magic. I can't get you out of my head. You are in my thoughts, my dreams, my mind, all the time. I want to be with you, Eloise.'

These were words she desperately wanted to hear, but they were also words that pulled her apart, so she took a step backwards, searching for her indignation.

'You want to be with me because you're a free agent,' she said with a shake of her head. 'But you don't care about me. You don't care about the bomb you'd be throwing into my life. How could I look at Elana again? How could I advise her to marry you? And if I did, and she became your wife, how could my friendship with her endure? Can't you see what you're asking me to do? To betray? To give up?'

'But what would you get in return?'

'What are you offering?' she spat angrily, waving a hand through the air. 'A night with you? Two? A secret, shameful affair that neither of us could ever speak of? And for that, you'd expect me to betray my dearest friend?'

He made a dark sound of irritation. 'I'm asking you—' He shook his head. 'This isn't going away,' he said firmly. 'I thought spending time together would help. It hasn't. The more I see of you, the more I need. I am on fire, little one, and only you can help me.'

She wanted to absorb the words. To allow them to soak in and become a part of her, but she was terrified of the consequences, terrified of the fissures that would form in her world.

'You're a free agent,' she said with a shake of her head. 'Choose someone else.'

'You're being deliberately argumentative now.'

'I'm arguing with you, yes, but not because I want to. Because what you're suggesting is so preposterous, so wrong…'

He closed the space between them, his hands capturing her upper arms, bringing her to him, so their bodies melded and their faces were just inches apart. 'Does this feel preposterous and wrong, *habibi*?'

Her legs trembled with enough intensity to make standing difficult.

'Do you want me to let you go?'

Say yes. Tell him to stop.

'Tariq,' she groaned, because it felt *so* good to be held by him, so good to be this close. Her heart was rabbiting in her chest, threatening to pull her apart. 'I can't do this.'

His nostrils flared and his jaw remained clenched. Despite what she'd said, she moved slightly, her body soft against his hardness, needing to feel every inch of him, then shivering when she succeeded. His arousal was unmistakable, and it called to her, so she bit back a sob.

'I know,' he said, finally, dropping his head so their foreheads were touching and breath mingling. 'And that makes me want you all the more.'

She closed her eyes, inhaling his intoxicatingly masculine fragrance, before he dropped his hands and stepped back.

'Go to bed, little one. I will not disturb you. You have my word.'

It wasn't just the noise that broke her sleep, but the immediate recollection of Tariq saying that he and his father would come to the mountains to hunt. The question occurred to her far too late: to hunt what?

The sound outside the window of her bedroom was unmistakable though. An animal. Large enough to crack tree limbs.

She sat bolt upright, staring at the window

first, and then towards the door, heart in her throat as she threw back the covers. She had no thought for her state of dress—she wore only the tunic Tariq had provided, but it was swimming on her smaller frame, so kept falling down one shoulder, revealing an expanse of creamy skin, her arm and the top of her breast. She rushed to the door and pulled it open.

Tariq was awake, moving towards the window of the kitchen.

'What is it?' she whispered, eyes huge in her face.

He cast a glance over his shoulder then turned back to the window. He concentrated on the darkness beyond the cabin and then signalled for her to join him. Belatedly, she recognised the gun at his side, a rifle, and she wondered how the sight of something she actively despised could somehow seem so distractingly erotic when paired with a man like Tariq.

'Come and see.'

Her fear had evaporated at the sight of the Sheikh. Not because of the gun, because he looked like someone who could tackle a bear, or a tiger, or whatever the heck was outside with his bare hands.

She looked through the window, beyond their reflections. Only one candle was lit, but it was enough to cast a distracting amount of light. 'Do you mind if I blow this out?' she asked, leaning closer to him.

He lifted the candle and extinguished it, plunging them into darkness. With that, came a rush of awareness of all of her other senses. She could *feel* his blood pumping. She could hear it. His breath was like a marching band. She tilted her face towards him, and even though it was now almost pitch-black in the cabin, she could *see* him as clearly as if the sun was right in the middle of the room.

'Look,' he said, but his voice had changed, gone lower, deeper, his tone gruff. 'Out there.' He moved behind her, lifting a hand to guide her attention, but now all she could focus on was the feeling of his body wrapped around hers. It was mesmerising and perfect.

She tried to control her breathing, but everything was rushing out of her, tumbling with panic and excitement and raw, undeniable need.

'What am I looking for?' she whispered.

'Over there.' He bent his head down to her level, so it pressed to her shoulder, and now she forced herself to concentrate, to look where he was looking, until she saw something shining in the clearing just beyond the car. Two gemstones, at hip height.

'Eyes!' She said, gasping.

'Tiger's eyes,' he said quietly.

'A real tiger? Here?'

He nodded, the gesture moving his face closer, so their cheeks brushed, and she closed her eyes a moment, savouring the feeling.

'An Arabian tiger. They're endangered in these parts. We use these mountains as a sanctuary, a breeding ground for them.'

'So there are lots here?'

'Not as many as there should be, but the population is growing year on year.'

'And you didn't think to warn me?'

'What for? You were never in danger.'

She shivered. 'Says the man with the gun.'

'He can't come into the cabin,' Tariq pointed out. 'You're perfectly safe.'

'And if he's still there in the morning?'

'He won't be.'

'You sound way more confident than I would be.'

'It's not my first night in the cabin.'

She turned a little, but it was a mistake, because their faces were so close, and this brought them closer. It almost brushed their lips together. She sprung back a little, jabbing her hip on the kitchen bench in the process. 'Did the tiger wake you?'

'I wasn't asleep.'

'It's two in the morning.' She'd checked the time before scrambling into the lounge room.

'I wasn't tired.'

Eloise tried not to read into that statement. She tried not to hope he might have been thinking about her.

'And now I'm wide awake.'

They stared at each other across the small space between them. Every breath was painful. Every moment she resisted him was an agony.

A moment later, there was a familiar sound— the striking of a match—and the candle was relit. His eyes lifted to hers, boring into her, his face set in tense lines as he studied her as if looking for an answer.

She stared back, confounded and confused.

He stepped forward, and she held her breath. He reached out, slowly, eyes on hers, until his fingers connected with her bare shoulder, then ran lower, catching the fabric of the caftan and pulling it higher, back into place. She swallowed past a lump in her throat.

'It's too big,' she explained unnecessarily.

He dipped his head, agreeing, but also, moving closer. 'Just a little.'

The thing swum on her.

'If you were not working for Elana, what would you be doing?'

'I don't know,' she whispered, wondering why the question hurt so badly.

'There must have been something you wanted to do, before coming to Ras Sarat.'

She contemplated that. 'As a child, I wanted to be a dancer.'

'You are very graceful.'

She smiled softly. 'I loved it. I would dance for hours and hours. I think it was a form of escapism. My ballet teacher used to let me stay and help her, even after my lesson had finished. Mum and Dad frequently forgot to pick me up anyway, so Miss Melanie would drop me home afterwards. I could dance for hours and hours and never get tired of it.'

'You didn't pursue it professionally?'

'It's not an easy job to get,' she pointed out. 'But in any event, once my parents died, my great aunt raised me, and she didn't approve.'

'Of dancing *or* horses? The philistine,' he said lightly, but his body was so close, and she saw the disapproval on his face. He was trying to make her feel better, but he was angry.

'I know. What a neglected childhood.'

He lifted a hand to her shoulder again, touching her through the fabric of the caftan, a frown on his face. 'You should have been able to keep dancing.'

'I did dance. In my room, when no one was looking.'

'I would like to see.'

Her throat felt strangled. 'I don't dance anymore.'

'Why not?'

'I grew up.'

'You deserve to dance.'

She shook her head and emotions bundled through her, making her eyes sting with salty tears. 'Don't, Tariq.'

'Don't what? Tell you the truth?'

'It's *not* the truth. Those were childish dreams. I grew out of them. I studied law and economics. I graduated with honours. I moved on. This is my life now.'

His hand dropped to her waist, holding her there, and she couldn't help but contemplate how *right* his touch felt. How perfect and simple and true.

'Working for the Crown Princess of Ras Sarat, advising her, strategising her marriage. These are noble pursuits, but what of your life and dreams?'

'Why can't this be my dream?'

'Because you're more than this.'

'Don't. Don't belittle who I am and what I do. I like my life.' She lifted her shoulders and the caftan slipped down again, revealing her creamy skin.

He was quiet a moment and then, slowly, oh, so slowly, he dropped his head. 'I'm glad.' His lips brushed her bare skin and she felt as though she'd been electrocuted. A thousand blades of lightning flashed inside her veins. She lifted a hand and clutched his shirt, holding on for dear life.

'For some reason I cannot explain, your happiness has come to mean a lot to me. I like to think of you having everything you want in life.'

She couldn't tell him, she didn't dare, that she would *never* have everything she wanted in life. She couldn't. Her best friend would marry the man she'd fallen head over heels in love with, and there was nothing Eloise could do about that.

CHAPTER NINE

WHEN EVENTUALLY TARIQ fell asleep, he had the nightmare. The same nightmare that had tormented him for years. He was drowning, unable to draw breath, but this time it was worse, because he'd now seen Eloise in the distance, and she was struggling to breathe as well. She was drowning, just out of his reach, and no matter how hard he kicked through the water, he couldn't get to her. His lungs were burning with the effort, and his legs might as well have been weighted with cement, for all the use they were to him.

He swam harder, but the water churned, and then, she disappeared, so he ducked beneath the surface, reaching for her, looking for her, aching for her; she was nowhere.

He woke in a cold sweat, looking around disorientated and confused, until the events of the prior evening came rushing back to him: the landslide, their being trapped here, playing cards, his desire to kiss her, the boundaries she kept erecting, that he was forced to respect. The tiger, her shoulder, the feel of her flesh beneath his mouth, her responsive body curving towards his, her trembles and shivers, her warmth and softness.

How forbidden she was to him when all he wanted was to make her his, utterly and completely.

Would that cure his fixation?

Even as he thought that, he dismissed it. This wasn't just lust. It wasn't just desire. There was that, too, but he was fascinated by *her*. By everything about her. The childhood she described so carefully, omitting, he was sure, the worst details. Her school life, her professional choices, her hopes and dreams. He could listen to her talk all day, and yet, even that felt like a betrayal.

He could live with that.

He could sin and then spend a lifetime paying penance, if that was what was needed, but he had seen the angst in her face, when she'd pleaded with him to understand that she could not betray her friend in that manner. He couldn't ask her to weaken, no matter how spectacular it would be.

If he cared about Eloise at all, he had to protect her from those feelings. He had to be strong even in the face of the biggest temptation he'd ever faced. He had to control this.

And he would. First and foremost, he was Sheikh Tariq al Hassan, exalted leader of Savisia; he could control anything. This would be no different.

She had dressed carefully before leaving the bedroom, neatly folding the caftan and replacing it on the bed. Memories of the way he'd kissed her shoulder had haunted her dreams; the skin still tickled there.

She needed the armour of her own clothes.

Her hair she'd pulled into a loose ponytail, and on her feet, she wore a pair of dark socks of Tariq's. He was awake when she emerged, and the kitchen smelled like coffee and pastry.

'Good morning.' He too was dressed, the thobe he'd carefully removed and stored the night before wrapped around his body, but it didn't matter. Last night, she'd seen him without a shirt, and that imagery would be with her always.

He lifted his gaze to her and offered a tight smile. 'There's coffee in the pot by the stove, and pistachio buns too. My security detail will arrive in around ten minutes.'

Disappointment was like a rock, dropping to her toes. 'Ten minutes?' She fairly groaned the words and had to force herself to take a breath and calm her fluttering nerves. 'I'm surprised they were able to clear the road so quickly.'

'Apparently, the idea of their Sheikh being stranded in a cabin is a powerful motivator.'

Something occurred to her, something unpleasant and tricky to bring up. 'Tariq, when they arrive and see me here, won't they think—'

'No.' The word was uttered with confidence.

'They know I am a man of honour. No one will think anything.'

Her smile was ambivalent. 'And yet, it could have.'

'It didn't. Neither of us would have let it.'

Her eyes held his and then she looked away, not wanting to admit how close she'd come to creeping out again, to crouching beside the sofa and asking him, begging him, to kiss her.

'But what if they think—'

'They will think nothing,' he said more firmly. 'And even if they were to think it, they would certainly not say it. My security guard is made up of experienced servicemen. Their discretion is expected.'

She pulled her lips to the side, hoping he was right. She didn't want Elana to hear of anything like this. It would be too hard to explain, and the last thing she wanted was to hurt her friend.

'Are we going back to the capital today?'

'I am. My flight will leave as soon as I get to the airport. Someone from my guard will drive you across country. It should take most of the day.'

She stared at him, her heart strangling in pain. 'I see.'

'I presume this is what you'd prefer?'

How tragic was she? Even given her fear of flying, she'd prefer that to driving, if it meant an extra hour with him.

'I suppose it makes sense,' she admitted begrudgingly, not holding his eyes.

'That was my thought.' He sipped his coffee, eyes lingering on her face a moment. 'I've given instruction that marriage negotiations will resume tomorrow.'

He wasn't being deliberately cruel, she was sure of it, but Eloise felt as though she'd been punched in the gut, and badly winded. All the warmth drained from her face and unconsciously, she took a step forward, her fingers pressing to the edge of the kitchen bench for support. Everything between them had changed. He was walling himself off from her, pushing back any intimacy they shared, treating her like…a stranger. It was courteous but so cold, and it almost killed her to feel that from him.

'Tariq, what's happened?'

His eyes met hers, something stirring in their depths. 'What do you mean?'

'You're being so…'

She stared at him, searching for words, for how to finish her sentence, but everything was shifting and she could no longer tell what was real and what was fantasy. What if she'd misunderstood everything? What if he'd been flirting with her for fun? To entertain himself on an otherwise boring evening? What if he did this sort of thing all the time? What if it had all been a lie?

And so the walls he was erecting somehow extended extra bricks and reached out to wrap around her as well, offering her protection she badly needed. She straightened, squaring her shoulders and staring at him with a carefully controlled expression.

'You're right,' she said, instead. 'This is for the best.'

Oh, so briefly, surprise shimmered in his eyes and then he nodded. 'Help yourself to some refreshments.'

She ground her teeth together, hurt and smarting. But to hide those feelings, she stalked into the kitchen and poured herself a coffee, heart bruised and aching.

She only had a chance to take two sips before a large four-wheel drive trekked through the woods, covered in dust. Six men in military uniforms jumped out, and a moment later, another four-wheel drive pulled up.

'The cavalry's here,' she murmured, casting a glance over her shoulder. But Tariq was already gone, moving towards the door, without a backwards glance.

The next day, still tired and a little stiff from the drive, she took her seat at the foot of the negotiation table, watching as Tariq, in the centre, listened to the advisors on both sides, nutting out details that had more to do with trade and financial agreements than it did marriage.

She looked at him more often than she should, willing him to look at her, willing him to *see her*, but always, she was disappointed.

It was as though they'd never met.

As though she was any other member of the Ras Sarat delegation, and his treatment of her hurt like the devil.

The meeting stretched into the afternoon, and she sat through it all, switching off her mind and heart and forcing herself to take an almost out of body perspective on this, to act purely in Elana's interests even when her heart was slamming into her and her stomach was in knots.

At one point, around four o'clock, she lifted a hand and absentmindedly kneaded the sore flesh at the back of her neck. Only then did Tariq turn to her swiftly, eyes narrowed, assessing the gesture, missing, as it turned out, nothing. Her hand dropped away quickly, her eyes fell to the table and her skin lifted in goosebumps. Blood flushed her body and her cheeks went a vibrant pink. For the rest of the meeting, she sat perfectly still, as though a magic wand had been waved, turning her to stone.

It had been a long day and Tariq was at the end of his patience.

He was doing the only thing he could, but ignoring her was a form of hell on earth. She hadn't spoken. Not once. Not even when he'd craved the sound of her voice or wanted her input badly. She'd stayed resolutely silent, occasionally making notes or frowning as if she disagreed with an opinion that was being put forth, but not venturing a counter viewpoint of her own.

He'd felt hatred then. Not for Eloise, but for his family and his role in Savisia and the duty that was on him to marry someone royal, to have royal children quickly. Hatred for her loyalty to a friend he barely knew, hatred that she wouldn't lower her scruples and enter into a short, wonderful, affair.

They both knew he would marry Elana, but why did that mean they couldn't be together in the interim?

He knew the answer, of course he did, but his ego, his libido, weren't satisfied by it. Nor was something else, something indefinable and urgent, a part of him that he couldn't comprehend but was jumping up inside of him, telling him to hell with the expectations and obligations on him, to hell with what his father would expect him to do: Eloise was right there, he could reach out and grab her, keep her here in Savisia with him, kiss her until she saw sense, until she begged him to make love to her.

And then what?

Have her wake up and hate him?

For all that he could use their physical connection to overcome her defences, he'd never do that. It was beneath him.

She had to come to him willingly.

She had to want him more than she wanted to fight this.

Or it would always be something he regretted.

And she'd made it abundantly clear she was going to fight temptation with her dying breath.

However, resuming wedding negotiations and forcing her to sit through them had been a low move. He felt that with every single minute of the day. She was so strong, so determined not to show any emotion, yet he felt it resonating off her, and more importantly, he felt it within his core. He judged himself, and yet he didn't call off the meetings again. He couldn't. This was the path of his future, he'd committed to it, and there was nothing that could stop it now. He would marry the Crown Princess of Ras Sarat, no matter how badly he wanted a completely different future.

The next morning, Tariq was preparing for the meetings when he received a call from his private secretary.

'Go ahead,' he muttered, taking a sip of scalding hot coffee.

'I'm aware your day is already scheduled, Your Highness, but I've had an interesting request.

Something I wanted to run by you before responding.'

That was, in and of itself, unusual. 'Yes?'

'Have you heard of Graciano Cortéz?'

'Of course. The property developer.'

'In fact, he is also an investor in many industries but primarily, he is known for his development work.'

'What about him?'

'He intends to buy a large amount of land in the city and convert it to hotel accommodation. He's asked to meet with you.'

'I hadn't heard anything about this.'

'It's all happened in the last two days.'

He closed his eyes, trying not to think about where he was two days ago, and how much he'd give to be back in the cabin with Eloise and her delicious, soft, creamy skin. His gut rolled and something in the middle of his chest ached.

'Why does he want to meet?'

'I suppose because of the scale of the development. I can make up an excuse, of course.'

'No, I'd be interested to hear his plans. I'll make the time. Schedule it in for today.'

'Thank you, Sheikh. Good luck with the negotiations.'

Tariq hung up the call, then swept from the room with determination and blinkered vision.

He wouldn't think about Eloise today. Only Elana, and the necessity of this future.

'Are you deliberately using the blandest words you can think of?' Elana pestered, so Eloise cringed. Bland was not how she could ever describe Tariq.

'Not at all. I just don't want to colour your thoughts on him. You'll meet him soon enough and you'll know how you feel.'

'Okay, fine, but what do you feel?'

Eloise almost choked on her pomegranate juice. 'I feel nothing,' she said quickly, the words strange in her throat.

'So I'm going to marry a guy and you have no idea if he seems nice or has three heads or kills cats in his spare time?'

'Actually, he does hunt,' she said, relieved when Elana laughed.

'I'd be surprised if he didn't. What else?'

'Ellie, I can't,' she whispered, looking down the hall at the increased action. 'He's coming now.'

'Call me later. Promise?'

'Yeah, I promise.' She disconnected the call, feeling like the worst friend in the world. The feeling only intensified as Tariq approached and her eyes seemed incapable of tearing themselves away from him. He walked with such confidence, flanked on either side by members of his cabinet. As he drew near the boardroom, his gaze travelled to her, met hers, then briefly flashed over her body, so a thousand arrows launched through her veins, but then he looked away, and moved beyond her.

Ice filled her body; she hated him then. How could he turn off from these feelings?

It just proved that she'd been right to resist him.

He hadn't really wanted her. He hadn't really cared for her. He'd wanted to sleep with her but when she'd refused, he'd accepted it and had obviously already moved on.

She hoped her heart would do the same thing.

'We've made good progress this morning.' His eyes encompassed the group, lingering, perhaps, a moment longer on Eloise than anyone else, but barely, so she was sure she was the only one who noticed it. Her shoulder tingled, as if he were kissing her there again; she looked away.

'I have another matter I must attend to. Please carry on without me. I'll check in this afternoon.'

Everyone stood respectfully, bowing as he walked from the room. Eloise stared at him in consternation. Ever since that morning in the cabin, she'd felt as if a part of her was being dragged from her body, a limb, an organ, something vital and essential.

That feeling compounded as he left the room.

She took her seat again and tried to focus, but her mind was, from that moment on, split in two directions.

Graciano Cortéz was a man whose reputation well and truly preceded him. He was one of the wealthiest men in the world, his developments known for their flair and appeal. He was environmentally conscious, culturally respectful, and made a point of employing local workforces as much as possible, meaning an investment by him in Savisia was a tantalising prospect.

Therefore, Tariq knew he should bring more of his focus to the meeting but unfortunately, he was no longer capable of doing any such thing. A part of him was always with Eloise, studying her, thinking about her, wondering about her, missing her. Fortunately, Tariq al Hassan on a bad day was still incisive and intelligent.

He strode into the ornately formal sitting room, eyes taking in the guards first and then, the man at the centre of the room.

'Graciano Cortéz?' he queried, moving close enough to extend his hand.

The Spaniard stared at it, and then lifted his eyes to Tariq's, causing the Sheikh a moment of confusion. Had they met before? There was something in the other man's eyes that was completely familiar.

'Your Highness,' Graciano said with a curt nod, belatedly reaching out and taking his hand. 'Thank you for meeting with me.'

'I was interested to hear of your development. I'd like to know more.'

'I have all the information over there, but that's not why I requested this meeting.'

Curiosity moved through Tariq. 'Isn't it?' He moved away a little, giving him some space to observe the other man's body language. 'Then why don't you enlighten me.'

Something was bothering Cortéz. He paced the room from one side to the other, then stopped abruptly, dragging a hand through his hair in a gesture Tariq found strangely familiar, before turning to Tariq with a look of uncertainty.

'You don't remember me.'

Tariq was careful to give nothing away. 'Should I?'

The other man's features shifted, disappointment obvious. 'No. You were too young...'

Something like adrenaline prickled along the back of his neck.

'Have we met?'

'You could say that.'

'I meet a lot of people,' Tariq said after a pause.

'I'm sure you do.'

'Is it important that I remember?'

Graciano's laugh lacked humour. 'I was hopeful.'

'I'm sorry to disappoint. Now, your development—'

Graciano's eyes flared, irritation obvious now. 'I came to talk to you about your family.'

It was like being speared by a bolt of lightning. The sensational words seemed to ricochet off the walls, making Tariq's heart feel as though it were breaking into pieces.

'That will be all,' he dismissed his guards with a curt nod, waiting until the room was empty save for the two men, then turning back to Graciano with the full force of his attention.

It was possible Graciano meant the Sheikha and late Sheikh.

Possible that Tariq was jumping to the wrong conclusions.

'What exactly did you want to discuss?' Tariq said, his voice emerging cool and level.

'What do you know of your parents?'

He stiffened. 'My parents are—'

'Dead,' Graciano interrupted, but gently, sympathy in his features. 'They died when you were a baby. It was a car accident. You are aware of this?'

Tariq was careful not to betray his feelings but inside, a part of him was crying out, tortured by what Graciano was saying, tortured and hurting.

'I think you should do the talking,' he said eventually, careful not to betray his feelings.

'If you wish.' Graciano dipped his head in a

nod. 'Your parents were killed. You were taken to a hospital, badly injured. It's a miracle you survived, in fact. I believe your adopted parents saw you, took pity on you, and brought you home with them, where you were nurtured back to health, cared for by the best doctors in the world, and raised as their own son. Of course, it was never intended that you would assume the throne. They simply fell in love with you and wanted to give you a better life. Am I right?'

Tariq's lips compressed in a grim line. So far as he knew, only four people on earth were aware of this: his mother, the doctor in Spain, Tariq and the prime minister of Savisia.

'Are you attempting to blackmail me in some fashion?' he asked, surprised, because everything he knew of Graciano Cortéz spoke of a man of integrity and honour.

'To blackmail you? Do you seriously think... To what end?' He looked bemused. 'Do you think I need the money?'

'I couldn't say. Why have you come here?'

'Because you were not the sole survivor of that crash. Are you aware of that?'

He was drowning again, a voice, a laugh, so familiar, so achingly familiar, a voice with no face. His dreams were all around him, memories haunting him, taunting him with their opaque, impossible to reach hold of quality.

'Who are you?'

'Graciano Cortéz,' he said quietly, moving closer. 'I am your brother.'

It wasn't true. It couldn't be. 'I have no brother,' Tariq said angrily, lying, because as Graciano spoke, fragments were piercing him, shocking him with their strength. 'My mother told me—she was told by the hospital—I was orphaned.'

'Orphaned, yes, but not alone.'

Tariq crossed his arms over his broad chest. 'Then why were we separated?'

'I cannot say, for certain. An accident? Or perhaps because of the donation your parents made to the hospital—it was very generous. I cannot speak for the motives of anyone else, but I am your brother. That much is fact.'

Brother. He groaned, dropping his head forward. He had been so young when the accident happened. He didn't remember his brother, and yet, he did. There was a sense enveloping him. A feeling of familiarity and comfort and, overwhelmingly, of love.

'My brother,' he said with a shake of his head.

'Look,' Graciano said, reaching into his wallet and pulling out an old photo, handing it to Tariq. He took it, but the force of recollection was so strong he almost blacked out. He gripped it harder, forced his eyes to focus. A man and a woman stared back at him, and two boys—one tall and gangly and the other just a chubby, dimply boy on his father's knee. He saw his own face, unmistakably, and the eyes that had been just out of reach all this time, those of Graciano Cortéz.

'Oh, my God,' he muttered, dropping his head. He was almost identical to the man in the photo, their features so similar, their skin darker than the other two, their hair thick and black. 'This is me.'

'That's us,' Graciano said. 'I have looked for you, from as soon as I had the means to do so. I have searched for you. But it was only recently that the truth was found—'

It brought Tariq back to the present, to his country, his people, his duties. 'How? How was the truth found?'

'I hired an investigator.'

'The adoption was a secret—everyone involved went to great lengths to ensure that it remained so.'

'You knew about this?'

'Not about you, but after my father passed away five months ago my mother told me the truth. I always felt that a part of me was missing. I always felt that there was something, someone, a part of me I couldn't make sense of,' he said with a shake of his head. 'It was all a lie. My parents were grieving in Spain—my mother had endured another miscarriage. They saw me, and they wanted to help me. That was all, at first. But days passed, with my mother coming to sit by my bed, and each day that went by without family coming to check on me made her certain she had to bring me home.' Tariq's eyes narrowed. 'My mother didn't mention you. I can't believe she knew about you—'

'Probably not,' Graciano responded with a small shrug. 'There was a lot of money involved. It would have been in the hospital's best interests to keep me out of the picture. I came to see you once, in hospital, but after that, I was forbidden. I thought I'd done something wrong, but it turns out, they just wanted to keep us apart.'

Tariq swore, handing the photo back, his eyes lingering on the faces. They looked happy. Warm. A family.

'Our father always said to me, "he's your responsibility. You must take care of him".' Graciano smiled wistfully. 'I adored you almost as much as they did. You were such a happy child—you smiled whenever we entered the room—but for me, it was different. You'd hold out your hands, wanting me to lift you up.' He laughed on a quiet exhalation and Tariq was jealous then, jealous of his brother's memories and knowledge of their family before this life. 'When I saw you in hospital, all broken and bruised, I wanted to take care of you with everything I was. But I wasn't allowed. I was too young to fight it, but I never stopped thinking about you, wanting to find you.'

'I have had nightmares,' Tariq said quietly. 'There was a voice. Your voice, I now realise. I couldn't see you, but you were there. I have had these nightmares for years, since I was a little boy. I thought it was because of the accident, but now I realise, it was my mind trying to make me remember. To look for you.'

Graciano moved closer, and they stared at each other for several moments before they embraced; two big, strong men wrapping their arms around each other, making the past disappear, so there was only this moment.

Emotion swamped Tariq.

There was love and anger and frustration and a total lack of comprehension. There was loyalty— to his birth parents and his adoptive parents, to his brother, to his people and kingdom, to his late, beloved father and the promise he'd made him, to care for Savisia with his dying breath. There was the realisation of how this news threatened that, because if Graciano knew, if an investigator knew, it was only a matter of time before this became more widely understood, and the threat to his reign was tantamount.

There was the crystallising of resolve, and an underscoring of the need of his marriage to Elana, and with that came despair, because he didn't want to marry her. He didn't want to be with anyone if it made it impossible for him to be with Eloise.

Everything swirled in a vortex. His past, present and the all-important future. The weight was immense.

He pulled away, keeping a hand curled around his brother's arm.

'The situation is complicated.'

Graciano's grin took his breath away because it was *his* smile. The same smile he'd known all of his life. He shook his head, wading through the mess of his life to admit that in this moment, there was good. The discovery of a sibling was a blessing.

'I anticipated you'd say that.'

'Can I rely on your discretion?'

'Do I seem like a man who shares his private life with the world?'

'Nonetheless, this is particularly sensitive.'

'I'm aware.'

'I'm not saying I won't speak publicly on this matter—I think that will be inevitable—but I need a little time to reflect, to speak to my mother and government first.'

'Naturally. I didn't come here to pressure you. Only, as soon as I knew where you were, I had to see you. I've looked for years...'

'I'm glad you came,' he said quietly, and it was the truth. It might have thrown a grenade into his life, but Tariq wouldn't have it any other way. 'Will you stay in Savisia awhile?'

'I'm here another week, for the development.'

'And then?'

'I'm based in London. But I can come back often.'

'London.' He nodded. 'There's so much I don't know about you. So much I want to know.'

'It's mutual.'

Tariq straightened, pulling away a little, needing to get his head around this. 'I'll have to take a couple of days to manage things here.'

'I can wait.'

CHAPTER TEN

SHOCK MORPHED INTO something else, something darker, as the day went on, and he tried to understand all the pieces of his life, all of the decisions and actions that had led him to this place in space and time.

He had been raised as a Savisian. The country was in his blood and bones, he would die for this place. And yet, he'd been born a Spaniard. He considered himself an only child and yet he had a brother, a brother he felt an immediate connection to, a brother he'd been denied for too long.

He had a future that was no longer in his hands. He had to marry Elana. Any hope of being able to find a way around it disappeared with the certainty that this news would soon be public—how could it not? If one person knew, it was only a matter of time.

Announcement of his engagement to the Crown Princess of Ras Sarat would calm most of the ruffled feathers and would placate those traditionalists who wanted to see a true royal baby on the throne of Savisia.

It would avert a possible civil war, or an uprising at least.

What would his father say if he were here?

He couldn't even seek comfort from that because his father had laid the groundwork for this. His parents should have made sure there were no other survivors before taking him. They should have thought before acting.

He stared around the boardroom, eyes landing on Eloise and lingering with a lack of control that bothered him almost as much as the rest of the day's revelations.

Her eyes lifted, straying to his, then jerking away, her lips parted.

Anger coursed his veins.

He was bobbing on a turbulent ocean, no anchor, no boat, no help in sight. Control was a faraway illusion. He needed to get away from this, from them. He needed to get far away.

Abruptly, he stood, scraping back his chair.

'That's enough.'

The room fell silent.

'We'll resume tomorrow morning. We're done for the day.'

The rest of the chairs pushed back, and one by one, the occupants bowed and left the room. Eloise was last. She lingered by the door, turning to face him, but in that moment, his anger was aimed even at her, because he needed her, and she was holding herself back from him.

He ground his teeth together, staring at her with ice in his veins.

'Are you okay?' she whispered.

Was he okay? Hell, he wasn't okay. How could he be?

He stared down his nose at her, eyes glittering in his face, focusing all of his anger at her because she was there and she'd let him down. She'd put Elana above him. He knew it wasn't a reasonable feeling to have, that she had shown loyalty and bravery in treating her friendship with so much respect, but what about her feelings for him, and his for her? What about what they owed each other?

'Why wouldn't I be?'

'You seem—'

'You are not here to psychoanalyse me, Miss Ashworth. I suggest you go back to your rooms and check in with your friend.'

She flinched and he felt his gut twist in response. Her eyes clearly showed her hurt. He'd done that to her, and none of this was her fault. His anger was totally unreasonable. But damn it, if they couldn't make love, they could make war—it was better to spark with her in anger than not at all.

But not if it made her feel like this. Not if he hurt her.

'Very well, Your Highness.' She curtseyed with that beautiful dancer's grace, and the moment she left the room he braced his hands on the edge of the table and dropped his head, feeling that he'd hit the low point, in that moment.

He'd pushed her away.

He'd sought to hurt her.

Why?

What had that achieved?

Why, when he wanted her with every cell in his body, had he thrown more barriers between them?

Something dark churned inside of him and suddenly, he was no longer thinking, but acting on instinct alone. He burst into the corridor, deserted except for a few members of the national guard, and looked left and right, searching for her familiar figure. He chose to walk left, striding the corridors with purpose until he rounded the corner and found her, walking with a frown on her face, eyes skimming the walls and barely registering the art that hung there.

He reached her easily but didn't touch her. He didn't dare.

'Would you come with me?'

She hesitated a moment. Wisely. Control was a long way back in his rear vision mirror.

'Come where?' It was hearing her voice that pushed him firmly over the edge, the sadness and resignation. The admission that she would go anywhere with him, no matter the cost. How he wished he could be the bigger person and release her from this hell of their creation, but his needs overpowered everything else.

'Into the desert,' he said, leaning down, his face just an inch from hers. 'But I should warn you, *habibi,* I am no longer able to honour the promise I made. If you come, I cannot tell you what will happen between us.'

She startled, eyes wide, face pale. 'Tariq, what is it?'

'Are you coming?'

Her lips parted, she swayed a little; still, he didn't touch her.

She stared up at him and he waited, nerves stretching, then finally, he turned, calling her bluff. He stalked away from her, not looking back, but hoping, hoping with all of himself, that she would follow.

She found him at the stables. Her lungs hurt from running, her heart was in tatters, and her knees were weak. Mostly, she was bursting with curiosity and concern. It was obvious that he'd reached a breaking point, and she couldn't fathom why.

'Tariq, wait,' she said, uncaring for the servants that were there, that heard her address him as a man, not as Sheikh. She couldn't.

His nostrils flared and with a short nod, the staff left the stables, giving her an interested look as they filed out.

'What's happened?'

He flicked a latch, opening a door for his stallion, who stepped out and made a guttural noise, tilting back his head.

'Are you coming?'

'This is madness.'

'I'm leaving now.'

'Wait,' she muttered. 'This isn't fair.'

'No, it's not. Ten seconds, Eloise. What's it going to be?'

'You can't do this to me.'

'Do this to you? Do this to *you*? What the hell do you think it's doing to *me*?'

She flinched and again, he felt like a total bastard, but he didn't care.

'I really hope you know what you're doing,' she said, eyeing the horse warily.

He crossed his arms. 'What does that mean?'

'Well? I can't get up there on my own.'

His eyes raked her and then he moved, fast and powerful, determined and in control, lifting her easily onto the horse. A second later, he was at her back and kicking the sides of Bahira, spiriting the beast out of the stables and away from the palace. He rode hard and fast, so she held on to the reins for dear life, but there was never any danger. Not with Tariq's strong arm around her waist, pinning her back against him, holding her there, needing her. She didn't know how she knew that, but she did.

He needed her, as much as he needed the desert and his freedom and some space from the palace and wedding negotiations.

Wedding negotiations. Her heart skidded and ached for Elana, for their friendship, for the decision she'd just made. As if he sensed it, he leaned closer, and doubt disappeared. Something more was between them, something that demanded *this*, whatever this was. She was at the whim of fate now, not thought, and it was a relief to let go and see what happened.

He rode like the wind. Sand whipped their faces; neither cared. He rode until they reached the rocky outcrop with the stream, he rode with the afternoon sun on their backs, warming them, and then, only once they were near the water, did he bring the horse to a halt and let himself breathe. But not think. Thinking would lead him to doubt and he refused to do that.

There was only one thing that would make this better. Not for good, but just for now, and that was enough.

He jumped off the horse and a moment later was grabbing her, drawing her with him away from Bahira to the large, ancient rocks that were flat and gently sloped. He moved quickly, sure footed on their surface after years of exploration. Around the corner, they levelled out and it was there that he stopped, turning to face her with nostrils flaring, thobe blowing in the gentle breeze.

She stared up at him, so trusting, face so calm, and then he groaned, passion almost eating him alive.

'Damn you,' he said, shaking his head because of all the women he could want with this passion, why did it have to be her? Why now? Perhaps if they'd met years ago, if his father had been alive and the truth of his adoption not remotely on his radar...but fate was cruel, and this was how things were.

'Damn *you*,' she responded, lifting her hands and pushing at his chest. 'Damn you.'

He caught her wrists, holding them there, and it was like being stung by a swarm of bees. Every cell in his body reverberated. Her breath was ragged, and he understood, he knew what she was feeling because it was burning him alive as well.

'I have to marry her,' he said, the fact something he couldn't ignore. 'I have to marry her.'

A tear glistened on her lash line and then fell down her cheek, rolling slowly before splashing to the ground. He stared at the silvery line it left on her face and honestly thought he could have punched something then. Her grief would be with him always.

'I know,' she whispered, though she didn't. How could she understand the new imperative that was at his back?

'But this is... If we don't... I will always regret...'

She sobbed then and nodded, the palm that was pressed to his chest curling in his clothes. 'I know.' She trembled. 'Me too.'

It was all he needed. They both understood what this was. A one-off. One chance, one time, so that they wouldn't look back and wonder and wish.

'No regrets,' he said emphatically.

'No.' But her tears were falling and it was more than he could bear. He kissed her then, hard and passionate, filled with all the dark emotions that were swirling through him, with the feelings that were rioting in his gut, with his need for her and his feelings for her, feelings that went beyond lust, that were knitted into stranger, heavier parts of his soul.

He kissed her like she was a delicate vase at first and then he kissed her as an equal, ancient and primal sensual desire controlling his every impulse. He tasted the salt of her tears and did everything he could to drive them from her heart and mind, so that only pleasure sustained her.

They stripped their clothes in unison, a frantic tangle of hands and fingers and limbs moving, shucking fabric from skin until they were naked, their bodies wrapped together, his pulling her to the stone, careful to place her on his discarded robe, to save from the cold hard edges of rock, but she didn't notice, didn't complain, only lifted onto her elbows to seek his mouth, to kiss him back, hungrily, needing, with the same abandon of sense and logic that had corrupted him completely.

His life had fundamentally changed and yet this, with Eloise, was the only thing that made sense. 'Damn you,' he groaned, but it wasn't her he was angry with, so much as everyone else. None of it mattered though. Not when her body writhed beneath his and her legs parted, silently inviting him to take her, to be with her. How could he refuse? How could he doubt the perfection of this? The hunger he'd felt since that first day had grown and grown so he thrust into her and almost exploded with the pleasure of that fulfilment. It took a monumental effort to bring himself back from the edge, to stop from coming right there, as her muscles tightened around him and welcomed him in euphoric completion.

She scraped her nails down his back and cried his name, filling the afternoon sky with the proof of her madness, of their madness, and he kissed her harder, tasting that pleasure, hearing it in his soul, aching for her even as he moved within her. It wasn't just her body he wanted but her total surrender to him, her admission that she was all his, and always would be. What an ass. Even in that moment of abandon he recognised what an awful thing that was to want—he would be married to another woman, sleeping with her, making her pregnant, yet he wanted Eloise to put her life on hold and pine for him always?

It was cruel and unfair but it was also human instinct—his instinct.

It was what he might have done if their positions were reversed.

He pushed the thought aside, terrified by it, by everything that was happening between them, even as he knew the experience was building him up, making him a different man, a stronger man, the man he was born to be.

'Tariq, I'm—I need—' He knew what she needed though. He understood her on some soul-deep level. He moved them in their own unique dance, his body anticipating and delivering, until she was trembling and falling apart and then he dragged his mouth all over her skin, flicking her, tasting her, tormenting her, bringing her back to the brink again, and then again, until the fourth time when she exploded and he went with her, wrapping an arm behind her back and lifting her up, so they were melded completely, not a hint of space between them as they shared the richness of that moment, as they found the fulfilment of release as if they were one person, not two, on very different paths.

'What happened, Tariq?' She shifted beneath him, ever so slightly, pinned as she was between him and the hardness of the rock.

'Is it not self-evident?'

She pushed aside his flippant response. This was not a flippant moment. 'What happened to upset you?'

His lips compressed and a muscle throbbed at the base of his jaw. She lifted a finger to it, touching him gently, then shifting her touch sideways, to lips she'd wanted to reach for since she'd first laid eyes on them. Doing so now was crazy and liberating. She refused to reflect on how temporary this state of freedom was.

He wasn't hers, and having slept with him, every single anchor point in her life had shifted.

She was adrift, but for right now, there was Tariq, and she would make the most of it, just for a little longer.

He expelled a sigh, pulling away from her so her body thundered with a silent complaint, but he only rolled onto his back then brought her to his chest, reaching for his discarded shirt to cover them a little. She smiled against his skin despite the heaviness that was dragging at her.

This moment was one of the few in life that was absolutely perfect. She closed her eyes and breathed in, waiting for him to speak, her fingers tracing idle, hungry paths over his chest.

'When I was just a baby, I was in a bad car accident.'

She lifted up, propping her chin on his chest so she could see him better.

'My body was broken—doctors thought I would die.'

She frowned, the hand that had been tracing lines over his chest coming to rest against his heart, feeling the sturdy beating with gratitude now. She didn't want to contemplate what could have happened.

'My recovery was slow. It wasn't certain that I would ever have full mobility or strength, but the doctors were wrong. I learned to walk, and then to run. To run fast and hard. My father was determined that I would be strong, much stronger than anyone else. He wanted me to be unbreakable.'

She felt his heart and knew that it was the case. Tariq al Hassan had been rebuilt, and he was everything he'd just said.

'He taught me to ride horses, to swim miles, to walk this desert as though it were the greenest grass in the world. He taught me to climb mountains, to move rocks with my bare hands, to fish and to hunt. He taught me to ignore pain, to endure just about anything.'

She made a soft noise because it was all so evident. When she looked at him, that strength was exactly what she saw.

'There is a legend about the sheikhs of this land, about the iron that fills our blood that makes us more than mere mortals. Borne of warriors, destined to take our place on the throne, to rule with the kind of compassion that can only come from an unbreakable commitment to what's right. I'm simply one in a long line of men like me.' He tilted his face to hers, eyes boring into hers. 'Only I'm not.'

She frowned. 'I don't understand.'

'After my father died, I learned the truth—he hadn't wanted me to know, but my mother wasn't comfortable with that.'

'What truth?' she pressed urgently.

He was still a moment, contemplative and then nodded, as if committing this to himself. 'I'm adopted, Eloise.' He waited for those words to filter through to her. 'My biological parents died in the accident that injured me so badly. Until today, I believed I was alone, that the accident left me an orphan. No parents, no siblings, just me.'

She pulled up closer to his face, urgency drawing her eyes together. 'What happened this afternoon?'

'My biological brother came to see me.'

She gasped, lifting a hand to her mouth. 'You have a brother?'

'I don't remember him.' He frowned. 'And yet somehow, I do. I felt a link to him immediately.'

'But…you're angry about this?'

He expelled a breath. 'No, not about discovering a brother. Eloise, don't you realise what it means?'

She furrowed her brow.

'I'm not royal. My place in this country, on the throne, it's all predicated on a lie.'

She shook her head, rejecting that outright. 'You might not be the biological son of the late sheikh but you were born to this. You are strong and powerful, smart, wise, kind, all the things that are necessary for a role like yours, all the qualities you just listed as being required by your customs.'

'But I am not royal,' he stressed adamantly, and finally, the penny dropped.

'And Elana is,' she said with a soft gasp. 'That's why you proposed this marriage.'

'Not only is she royal, many generations ago, our bloodlines were of the same royal lineage. Her heir would sit on the throne of Savisia, and this would negate any discontent. It would avert a civil crisis—most importantly, it would right the wrong of my parents' decision.'

'What your parents did was save a boy who needed saving.'

He shook his head. 'They should have told me the truth.' He closed his eyes, features showing anger.

'For years, I have had this single nightmare,' he said quietly. 'I didn't realise it, but when my mother told me the truth, I realised immediately. It is a strange memory, not of anything specific, just a familiarity I have with someone, something else, somewhere else. I was only nine months old, but somehow, a part of that life is imprinted on me, a part of me; it's as though I've always known I was different, that something was wrong. All my life this nightmare has tormented me. Now I believe it is my past, trying to be known. I just didn't realise there was something I needed to reach out and grab.'

She felt sympathy for him, not just that his parents had concealed the truth from him, but also because his world had been rocked to the foundations. Because he'd lived with this for five months, worrying about the political fallout from a deeply personal situation.

'How do you know there'd be a crisis?' she asked gently. 'Even if anyone found out...'

'People will find out. My brother's appearance

changes everything. Too many people know. The only way to handle this is to get ahead of the information with an announcement of my own.'

'And what? Forfeit your right to rule?'

'It should not be mine, by right,' he said sharply. 'If there were anyone else—'

'But there's not. You were born for this, raised for it, at least.'

'Yes. I was raised for it,' he agreed gruffly.

'And you're good at it. How can you even think of walking away—'

'I'm not. Don't you see? Everything we've been doing here has been to secure my place on the throne, not to abandon it. However I might personally feel about this, I owe the people of Savisia a great debt of gratitude. I cannot desert them—'

'You don't owe anyone anything,' she interrupted.

'There is no one else. A distant cousin has a claim on the throne, but he is far from a suitable fit. He would drive the economy into the ground within a decade,' he said with a shake of his head. 'If there were someone, anyone, else I would abdicate, but I can't. Don't you see? I was raised to fulfil this role and I cannot walk away from that.'

Eloise's eyes were awash with sympathy.

He continued with gruff determination. 'Marriage to Elana is politically necessary for me, and also, for her. The kingdom of Ras Sarat hangs by a thread, but Savisia is rich, powerful, with strong alliances and trading partnerships. Everything about this makes sense.'

'I know,' she whispered, because it did, and it was Elana's hope that the marriage would come to pass. 'That's why you have to marry her.'

'But then, there's you,' he said quietly. 'Can't you see how this complicates things?'

'No,' she groaned, heart breaking. 'We both know it can't.' The two people she loved most in the world had everything to lose if the marriage fell through—Eloise wouldn't be responsible for that.

Silence fell. It was too early for the sweet chorus of night birds. The sun was still high, the sky blue; the warmth of the day surrounding them, even when her heart was cold.

He reached for her fingers, lacing them through his. 'What if you were to stay in Savisia?'

Her heart stammered. 'How would that work?'

'Stay for me,' he said, his voice rumbling. She felt like she was in free fall.

'And your marriage to Elana?'

'Purely for the sake of a royal heir,' he said. 'That would be unavoidable. But beyond that, she would be nothing to me.'

Eloise's heart splintered. 'She's my best friend. You can't think I'd ever want that for her?'

'And what about you? What do you want for yourself?'

'This,' she pressed a hand lightly to his heart, 'is a poisoned chalice. The thing I want, the thing I want with all my heart, would ultimately destroy me because of what that selfish choice had cost my friend. I could never do it, and I think you know that.'

He swore softly. 'And you said *I* was running away?'

'I'm not,' she said quietly. 'I'll continue to serve Elana's interests from Ras Sarat. It's my home.'

'Stay here, Eloise,' he said with urgency. 'As a friend, if that's all you can offer.'

'That would never work,' she said thickly. 'Please don't ruin this moment by asking me to do something I cannot even contemplate.'

His features were etched with determination. 'You can do whatever you want. You're afraid.'

'Yes,' she agreed without hesitation. 'I'm deathly scared of hurting the friend who's been with me through thick and through thin, who would give her life for mine. And yet I'm here with you, doing exactly that. Don't ask for more.'

It was what she'd said in the cabin. She felt it as strongly now as she had then.

'You won't even think about it?'

It was anathema to her. Every cell in her body rejected the idea of an ongoing betrayal of Elana, and she knew that the marriage had to proceed. But she nodded slowly, because she was greedy for just a few more moments of beauty with Tariq, the last few moments she'd spend with him, ever. She wanted to drink this in, to nourish her soul, so that when she left—and she would leave—she would have something to sustain her through the long years ahead.

He alone would have her heart, for as long as it beat in her body, it would beat solely, always, for him.

CHAPTER ELEVEN

DUSK BREATHED ACROSS the desert, gentle and iridescent at the same time, electrifying the atmosphere. The stars began to twinkle and it was like the falling of a hammer. They both knew it was time to leave.

Eloise shifted first, moving her head from his chest, trying not to think about the future, about how much she'd miss him. She had to be able to live with herself, and only by leaving him could she achieve that.

A poisoned chalice indeed.

'Have dinner with me tonight.' His command curled around her, tempting her, making her doubt her firm resolution to end this now, before things could go further. Before she could weaken.

'I think that would attract the wrong kind of attention.'

His eyes flared. 'We've eaten together before.'

'It's different now,' she chided gently. 'Everything's different.'

His jaw shifted as he ground his teeth together.

'Tell me about your brother,' she said, changing the subject, as she reached for her clothes and began to dress. 'What's he like?'

Tariq's gaze faltered, shifting to the palace. 'Familiar.'

'Like you?'

'Like someone I've known all my life,' he corrected. 'His voice, his eyes, his smile, they're all pieces of me.'

'It must have felt…a thousand things, actually, when you met him.'

'It was surprising.'

Her lips twisted, and her eyes feasted, as he too stood, stretching first then bending, picking up his loose cotton shirt, cuffed pants, and finally, his thobe. Before he could replace it, he came to stand right opposite her, toe to toe, his eyes scanning her face. 'No regrets?'

Her heart shimmied like the sky overhead. She regretted much about their situation but strangely, not what they'd just done. 'No. None.'

His nod was one of approval and it warmed her heart.

They rode back to the palace slowly, and he stopped where he had the last time, away from the stables and the curious eyes of his staff.

'Wait here for me.'

She was tempted to fight that, to leave immediately, but she wasn't yet ready. Her heart was still hungry for him. Hungry for more.

She watched as he rode away, his back straight, achingly strong, and only then did she let a small sob break from her lips, a tear drop from her eyes. She lifted a hand and pressed it to her cheek, then spun her back, focusing on the desert sky behind the palace.

Minutes later, she couldn't say how many, his hands came around her waist, pulling her back to him, so she closed her eyes and inhaled, the familiar presence of his body now a part of her.

'I can come to you tonight. Later. I can rely on my palace staff for discretion.'

She turned in his arms and pressed a finger to his lips. 'Let's not argue about this, Tariq.' She dropped her finger away. 'You can't come to me, and I won't come to you. What just happened was a beautiful piece of unreality.'

His eyes flashed with something dark but he contained it quickly. 'Let's not argue,' he agreed. 'We can discuss this further another time.'

'Tomorrow,' she said with a small nod, knowing that tomorrow, she'd be long gone.

'Do you have a moment?' His tone really didn't invite argument, and he knew the woman sitting across the room could sense, even from that distance, that her son was angry.

She nodded towards her companions, smiling softly. 'Thank you, ladies, that will be all.'

Four elegant Savisian women filed from the room, and with another curt nod, the two remaining servants, leaving the Sheikh alone with his mother.

'Darling, have you eaten? There are some leftovers…'

'I'm not hungry.'

His anger was palpable and new. Though he was a man who felt strongly, he couldn't recall the last time he'd been angry like this. Not since he was a child. It wasn't his way. He was a problem solver, and always had been. When he saw something that needed fixing, he simply worked out how to fix it. Anger, he'd always said, was a futile emotion.

'Then come and sit. Tell me what's happened.'

He paced towards her but didn't sit. He crossed his arms over his chest and stared out of the window behind her.

'Did you know about him?'

'About whom, dear?'

'Did you know, when you took me, that I had a brother?'

Tariq did nothing at first to ease her discomfort, but rather, stared at her, reading her face like an open book. It was abundantly clear he'd just floored his mother.

'It's not possible,' she said after a long moment. 'We were assured you were the sole survivor. It's why we brought you with us. I couldn't bear the thought of you alone. We were assured everyone else had died, told that there was no one available for foster care—you were going to be placed in a home once you left hospital. *If* you left hospital. How could I have left you there, Tariq?'

A muscle jerked in his jaw; even his name was a wrenching discomfort to him. It was not *his* name, not the name he'd been given at birth, and yet it was who he was now. 'You were lied to.'

'It can't be.' Her downward lips showed how perplexed she was. 'Why would anyone do that?'

'You were prepared to donate a considerable amount in exchange for my quick adoption, were you not?'

Her eyes swept shut, all the colour drained from her face. 'The hospital was underfunded. Your father and I wanted to help.'

He could well believe their altruism.

She stood, agitated, fidgeting her hands. 'And naturally, given your father's place in the royal family, we wanted things to happen quickly and quietly.' She groaned, shaking her head in obvious distress. 'But if I'd known about your brother, I would never have—no, that's not right. I would have brought both of you. I would have wrapped him in my arms and carried him here, caring for you both.' She moved closer to Tariq. 'When I saw your little body in the hospital bed, all I could think of was your mother.' Her voice grew thick with tears. 'They say the pain of losing a child is the worst thing in the world.' She pressed her fingers to her chest. 'But the pain of a mother leaving a child, of not knowing how their child will be cared for, of missing all the milestones, of not being able to tuck her little one into bed at night, to laugh with you...' Tears fell down her face. 'The moment I saw you, I made your mother a promise in my mind. I would love you. I would care for you. I would make sure you lived a good, rich, wonderful life. I would give you everything their deaths had put in jeopardy. You were mine, Tariq, from that moment.'

It was impossible not to feel the truth of that sentiment, not to acknowledge that she had acted from a place of love.

'But in your haste to care for me, he was left behind. We were separated.'

She pressed her palm to her mouth. 'I had no idea.' She hesitated. 'I know it must be hard to believe me. We kept this truth from you for a long time.' A hint of anger coloured the words, anger, Tariq imagined that was aimed at his father, who'd been determined Tariq should not know about his birth. 'It was a decision we made out of love—we wanted to spare you the pain of feeling *different*. Then you'd have those nightmares, and I knew you were, somehow, re-membering the accident, that your little heart had watched your parents die in the most grue-some way, that you'd been trapped and unable to help them. Then, I wanted to save you from having to relive that. You were happy with us. We loved you so much, and you us. What good was there in stirring up the past by telling you about Spain?'

'Apart from the fact I had a fundamental right to know who I am?'

'Yes,' she whispered. 'Something I came to accept as you aged. For the most part, you are so like your father, but every now and again, I'd see a gesture or an expression, one I wouldn't rec-ognise, and I'd wonder about the people who'd given you life. But never once did it occur to me that you might have family that survived.'

'Well, my brother did.'

'How do you know?'

'Because this afternoon, I met him.'

She gasped. 'He's here? In Savisia?'

He dipped his head.

'Oh, my darling.' Her hand cupped his cheek, but she said nothing more.

'This will come out,' he said, gently, as if to warn her. 'Too many people know the truth now.'

She flinched. 'How do you feel about that?'

His nostrils flared. 'I would rather live with

the fallout than walk through any more lies. I'm ready for it, Mother. Are you?'

Dawn broke across the desert, the sky reassuringly familiar, even when all the major compass points of his world had shifted overnight.

He had replayed his conversation with Eloise over and over, analysing it from every angle, studying her facial expressions and the tone of her voice, trying to make sense of what she wanted and needed, trying to find an answer beyond the impossible to contemplate: that she wouldn't see him again.

There was one point on which he felt he could persuade her.

The prospect of her living in Savisia if he promised they wouldn't touch each other again. It was better to have her in his life in any capacity, as his own advisor, as a friend, than to lose her completely. While it was difficult to imagine that life, to imagine being near her and not wanting to have her, it would simply require discipline.

He was determined not to lose her, particularly not now, when his life was in such a state of flux. He needed her.

He dressed quickly, opting for a dark thobe without realising it—perhaps subconsciously he feared the worst?—then strode through the halls of his palace, until he reached his office. As soon as he arrived, he lifted the phone.

'Please have Miss Ashworth of the Ras Sarat delegation brought to me here as a matter of importance. We have business to discuss.'

He disconnected the call and began to wait, eyes practically burning a hole in the door in anticipation of her arrival.

Ten minutes later, there was a knock on his door and he braced for this moment, this conversation—one of the most important in his life.

'Come.'

He stood, aware of every limb and cell in his body. He grew hard with anticipation but schooled himself to calm down. After all, a lifetime of denial was about to begin. He hoped.

It was not, however, Eloise Ashworth who strode through the doors, but rather Jamil, his good friend and advisor.

'You,' Tariq grunted, crossing his arms.

'Good morning to you as well, Your Highness,' Jamil said with a hint of humour. 'You're up early.'

'I've been up all night, in fact.'

'Marriage negotiations?'

He flinched. The words felt like a betrayal. 'What are you doing here?'

'You asked for that woman from the Ras Sarat delegation to join you?'

'And you are not her,' Tariq pointed out.

'Not last time I looked.' Jamil grinned, clearly not reading the Sheikh's mood.

'Where is she?' It was early, Tariq reasoned. Perhaps she was still asleep and the servants didn't want to wake her. Even at his command? That seemed unlikely.

'She left last night.'

Tariq's heart ceased to beat. The world stopped spinning. Everything was frozen solid. Only his breath punctuated the room in harsh little spurts.

'That's not possible.' There had to be some mistake. Jamil didn't even know her name, he simply referred to her as 'that woman from Ras Sarat'. How much could he know about her?

'I helped arrange her transportation myself,' Jamil said casually, with no idea of the rage that was building inside Tariq. Rage without focus, just all-consuming, devastating rage. 'Apparently there was a conflict in her schedule. She was quite adamant she couldn't wait until this morning.'

She'd run away from him.

She'd fled.

She'd never had any intention of discussing their situation further. She'd left, without saying goodbye. He pressed his palms to the desk.

'The other delegates have remained. This shouldn't affect today's meetings.'

Tariq dropped his head, staring at the desk.

'Your Highness?'

Tariq didn't respond.

'Tariq?' Jamil was closer now, directly opposite the Sheikh. 'What's going on?'

But something occurred to Tariq, and he grabbed hold of it. 'Who was driving her?'

'I don't know. One of the royal guards. Why?'

'Find out who, and where they are. It's been what, ten hours of driving? That might have taken them close to the Savisian border, but probably not. And ready a helicopter.'

'Tariq, you're not making any sense.'

'No, I'm probably not.'

'The car drove her to the airport, where she had a seat booked on a commercial airline, to take her home.'

Tariq jerked his face up, eyes piercing Jamil. 'She *flew*?'

A thousand feelings erupted inside of him. Foremost, the realisation that she must have been absolutely desperate to escape to even contemplate flying, given the depth of her fear. And then, the thought of her up in the air, afraid, with no one to hold her, no one to tell her it would be okay, no one to care for her.

He groaned softly, spinning away from Jamil's

penetrating gaze, focusing on the lightening sky,
the dawn of a day that would not include Eloise.

He found himself in her suite shortly after that.
No one had cleaned it yet, and the air retained a
hint of her fragrance, so his gut twisted and hurt
as though he'd been punched hard.

He moved to her bed, and ran his fingers over
it, imagining her here, sleeping, turning, dreaming of him. To her bathroom, where there was
no sign of occupation, no toiletries remaining,
everything perfectly neat and tidy, to the lounge
room, and a little desk that overlooked the citrus grove. His eyes fell to approximately the spot
they'd stood in the first day he'd met her on his
horse and his gut jumped.

Slowly, he tore his eyes away, focusing on
the desk, where a single white, sealed envelope
was laid out, with his name written neatly on
the front.

Not his name, but rather his title, to give, he
presumed, the impression of the note containing
official business. He lifted and opened it in one
motion, fingers moving deftly.

T,
To stay in Savisia and be anything other
than what we were in the desert would be
a pain too intense to bear. To share you,

*to see you live your life publicly with any-
one else, to have a family with them—these
are things I want for you, but that I cannot stand by and witness. If I only loved
you less.*

*You will be a wonderful husband. Please,
take care of her.*
Best wishes always
E

He scrunched up the note, keeping it balled
in his fist, and stormed through the palace, face
darker than a storm cloud, eyes flashing lightning.

'But it's so far away,' Elana decried, and with
good reason. The two had always promised
they'd stay together, remaining inseparable until
they were little old grannies.

'It's only a year,' Eloise said. 'The opportunity
came up while I was away and I knew you'd be
happy for me,' she added a teasing tone to her
voice, even though she was dying inside. The
flight out of Savisia had been traumatic enough,
let alone that she was leaving Tariq and any idea
of seeing him again. And now? Hours later, she
was telling her best friend that she was return-
ing to London to take up a fictional dream job,

simply because she couldn't bear to live with the guilt of what she'd done.

'I am, of course,' Elana said quickly, frowning. 'But—'

'You will have more than enough to occupy you in the coming months, Your Highness.'

Elana's face paled. 'Of course. My marriage.'

'Yes,' Eloise busied herself pouring tea rather than showing how the mention of such a marriage affected her. 'Your marriage, that's right. You'll be Crown Princess of Ras Sarat and Sheikha of Savisia. Your time will be well and truly taken up.'

'But how will I navigate all that without you?'

'You'll have His Highness,' Eloise said, and for a moment, she was glad for her friend, because Tariq was truly a wonderful person and he would be a good husband. She tamped down her own feelings, relegating them to the back of her mind.

'And you really think this is what I should do?'

'I think it's important for your kingdom,' she said quietly. 'And for his.'

'Will you at least stay until the wedding?'

'I'm so sorry...' Her voice faltered. 'They've asked for me to start as soon as possible. I was planning to leave today.'

'But you just got back!'

'I know. It sucks.'

'You're just too in demand, my dear friend. Do you have time to finish breakfast at least?'

She wasn't hungry, but she nodded anyway, reluctant to leave Ras Sarat and Elana, even when she knew she must.

He flew himself to the east, and drove to the cabin, noting the landslide had been largely cleared as he went. He needed to think. Space and time. He needed to be away from people, to get clarity and work out how to proceed. He had to pull emotion from the situation and see the facts as they stood. He needed answers.

In the cabin, he set to analysing all of the circumstances at play. His brother, Tariq's potential lack of suitability to sit on the throne of Savisia, civil uprising, Ras Sarat's finances, and finally Eloise. It was the last consideration that made the others seem irrelevant, but that wasn't so.

And he knew Eloise wouldn't see it that way.

She wanted him to marry Elana, for the sake of the kingdom of Ras Sarat. Any solution had to include a way to help that country.

And his own predicament?

How much was he prepared to sacrifice? How much could he gain?

He stayed in the cabin for two nights, and on the third morning, clarity shifted inside of him, as he began to see a better way forward. It would require the moving of many parts. The good will of almost everyone. But if he could succeed? He'd be king of the world.

He spoke to Mother first. 'I'm going to make a statement. This could be a bumpy time. I cannot say that there will not be civil unrest as a result, or perhaps another claim on the throne.'

Her lips pulled into a serene smile. 'You'll manage.'

That pulled him up short. 'Why are you so sure of that?'

She shifted in her seat a little. 'When we found you in that hospital bed, you were utterly destroyed. The accident had scrambled you all up. The doctors thought you wouldn't survive the first twenty-four hours, but you did. Then they thought you wouldn't last the week. They thought you might never walk and look at you now. You're a fighter, Tariq. You always have been. You have the strength of a thousand warriors at your back. And you'll always have me there, too.'

Graciano was next. Their second meeting was of a different nature, for the simple reason that he brought his family—a wife, Alicia, an eleven-year-old daughter and a toddler. Tariq suddenly felt his heart expanding to include this family, *his* family, his niece so like the mother Graciano had shown him in that photograph. It was only natural to include the Sheikha in the meeting, and she took such a shine to both Graciano and Alicia, the latter of whom was quite overcome at one point. Tariq saw tears glistening on her eyes and enquired if she was okay.

'Graciano and I were both alone a long time before finding each other,' she said quietly. 'Your mother is so welcoming, so loving. It's...been a lovely afternoon.'

Tariq had nodded softly. 'Would you mind sitting with her a moment longer? There is business I must discuss with your husband.'

'Your brother,' she said with a warm smile, then put an arm around him. Such a casual, unexpected gesture of affection, he found it quite natural to return it.

But when he looked at Graciano and Alicia, and saw their easy, obvious love, all he could think of was Eloise, and the desperate, aching yearn he felt to see her again.

The last visit he had to make was to Ras Sarat. Not to Eloise, though it almost killed him to fly into the country without planning to meet with her—yet. But there was no hope of a future with Eloise—to undo the poisoned chalice—without first speaking to the Crown Princess.

Knowing how much this woman meant to Eloise had him viewing her differently, as he entered the pretty sunroom a servant led him to.

Her Highness stood waiting, wearing an elegant green silk dress, hair pulled back in a low bun. Jamil was right, he realised. She was very beautiful, but nothing within Tariq stirred.

He bowed low. 'Thank you for seeing me.'

'Of course.'

Tariq was a man of his word, a man of honour, which was why the next conversation was one of the hardest he'd ever had to have. 'Your Highness, it is no longer possible for us to marry.'

Surprise etched itself on her features, but there was no disappointment. She stood right where she was, pretty features calm, head tilted, inviting him to continue.

'When you were still a child, this country was being driven into the ground by corruption and greed. The current state of affairs is not your fault.'

Now, she did gasp, and her cheeks coloured pale pink. 'Not my fault, perhaps,' she said with a small nod, 'but my responsibility.'

He admired her character greatly, then. She wasn't looking to avoid this: she wanted a solution. 'And marriage to me is indeed one way to help, but I have another.'

Urgency had her moving forward. 'What? I

don't mean to sound offensive, but marrying you was not something I would have considered if there were any other way. And believe me, I've looked.'

He laughed gruffly at her frank admission. Perhaps it was because she was so close to Eloise, but he liked her instantly.

'Have you heard of Graciano Cortéz?'

'Of course.'

'He had been looking to build an enormous investment—a series of hotels and five-star retail precincts—in the capital of Savisia. What if his plans changed, and instead, he built them here, in Ras Sarat?'

Her lips parted. 'But why would he do that?'

'Your country is beautiful,' he said with a shrug. 'Investment from someone like him will employ tens of thousands of people and generate billions of dollars in revenue. Most importantly, it will begin a rejuvenation, bringing renewed investment, tourism and attention. You will need to turn your attention to overhauling your country's financial regulation system, to be sure political operatives don't siphon off the profits—'

'That's already underway,' she said with a nod. 'Eloise, my friend—I believe you've met her?— she has been working with the parliament for the last two years on legislative reforms to prevent the corruption of the past.'

Of *course* she had been. A smile touched his lips as he imagined her wading through the laws, tweaking them, scrapping them completely where necessary, her unquestionable sense of rightness leading her to fight for what was right. And her loyalty to Elana.

'There are other ways my country can help yours,' he said gently. 'I regret that it's taken me so long to realise your plight. You shouldn't have to shoulder this worry alone. Savisia and Ras Sarat were always friends, and we can be again.'

She sat down, looking overwhelmed by the offer.

He continued, needing to reassure her, perhaps to salve his guilt. 'For example, we currently only get ten per cent of our imports from Ras Sarat. That could be made higher, closer to twenty-five per cent.'

'We'd need to scale up to that over the next two years, and I'd need a firm commitment from your government in order to begin that process.'

'Consider it done.'

She nodded, but slowly, her eyes roaming his face. 'What's happened, Your Highness?'

He didn't pretend to misunderstand her, but nor did he rush into explanations. He wasn't sure if it was his place.

'Eloise gave me the distinct impression that you and your people were determined for this marriage to happen. That it was best for everyone. The last thing I expected was to see you, only a few days later, urging the opposite.'

'Eloise was instrumental in bringing me to this point,' he said quietly. That was indeed the truth. 'Is she available to discuss some of these details?' He cursed how weak he sounded, but he'd been wrong to think he could come here and not see her. It was a marvel he'd made it through the last ten minutes.

'I'm sorry, no. But someone else from my delegation can step in, of course.'

He was trapped there. He stared at Elana, totally lost, caught between a rock and a hard place, wondering how to broach this without hurting the Princess's feelings, but needing to see Eloise more than anything else in the world.

'Your Highness.' She moved even closer, eyes scanning his face in a way that was unnervingly similar to Eloise. 'Something happened in Savisia, didn't it?'

He was very still, and utterly silent.

'Eloise came back ahead of the delegation. And she *flew*, which is shocking in and of itself, but then, she left almost immediately, once again, *flying* back to England. You have no idea how long it took her to get here originally because she refused to board anything that lifted off the ground.'

He would have smiled if he weren't battling the revelation that Eloise was no longer on the same continent as him.

'She values your friendship above all else,' he said, quietly, thinking, searching for the right words. 'She wanted you to marry me because she thought, as I did at the time, that it was the best way to serve your kingdom, and also meet my needs.'

'The marriage had some practical points in its favour, but I'm glad you suggested an alternative. I'm…not sure I could have lived with myself for making such a practical marriage.'

He lifted his brows. 'I didn't realise you were reluctant.'

'You weren't supposed to. Even Eloise didn't know the depth of my misgivings. If she had, she would have found a way to put a stop to it,' Elana said, and Tariq smiled, because her loyalty was fierce and strong.

'I spent a lot of time with Eloise while she was in Savisia. I determined early that she would be the person whose advice you would listen to, therefore, she was the only one I had to convince.'

'A wise interpretation of the situation.'

He dipped his head. 'However, there was a problem.'

She waited, silently encouraging him to continue.

'In spending time with Eloise, I found it impossible not to—' He stared at the princess, hating himself for having to have this conversation, worried he was doing something Eloise would never forgive him for. But everything he'd manoeuvred in the last few days had been to bring him to this point. 'I came to feel—' How could he explain it? What words would do justice to what Eloise had come to mean to him? 'I came to realise that I couldn't imagine my life without her in it. I fell in love with her.'

Elana stared at him and then, broke out into a smile. 'You love Eloise!' she said, clicking her fingers. 'Of *course* you do. How could you not? And she loves you! Why else would she have scampered away like that?'

He stood very still.

'She knew—or thought—that this marriage was my salvation. Perhaps she thought it was yours too. She wanted it enough for both of us that she was prepared to sacrifice her own happiness, to take herself completely out of the picture, rather than risk ruining it for us. That's so like her.' Elana's smile was watery. 'She is the most thoughtful, kind-hearted person in the world.'

'Yes,' he agreed without hesitation, feeling instantly bonded to Elana now that they were both on the same page: in complete adoration of Eloise. 'Tell me where I can find her?'

Elana grinned. 'But of course.' She moved to a desk and scrawled something out, then handed the paper to him. 'My home in London. I suggested she stay there while she found her feet with the new job, halfway hoping she'd hate it and come home before she'd signed a lease anywhere else.'

'She'll come home,' he promised, gripping the paper tight between his fingers. 'I'll make sure of it. Thank you, Your Highness.' He bowed.

'Please, let's not be so formal. We're like family now.'

Family. More family. He grinned as he left the room, on a quest to lock the last piece of the puzzle in place. There were still a lot of unknowns, but with Eloise, he knew he could stare each and every one of them down.

CHAPTER TWELVE

SHE READ THE Savisian newspapers each morning, looking for the announcement. For any *hint* of an announcement, telling herself that when she saw it in black and white, she'd exhale.

Then, it would be a *fait accompli* and she could stop questioning her decisions, looking for another angle, hoping for some way to have her cake and eat it too.

But the truth was, she could never do that to Elana. She couldn't do it to Tariq, either, nor the children they would have.

She wouldn't be a woman in the shadows, always on the periphery of their family. It was beneath her and so far beneath the loyalty Elana deserved.

Days passed, and still no announcement came. Texts with Elana revealed nothing new. Eloise grew restless. She knew she had to find work, something to occupy herself with, but she was suffering from a lack of energy.

She barely left the house. She went from the bed to the sofa to the kitchen to make a tea, then back to the sofa, and always, the events of her days in Savisia played in her mind like a film. Every interaction, smile, touch, closeness…

They played over and over, so her heart throbbed and twisted and she ached for him, desperately needed him, in a way that was making it impossible to breathe. But this was now the rest of her life.

She had to learn to live with this.

On the fifth day, she dressed in jeans and a sweater, determined to *do* something. She ate a small breakfast, had a strong, black coffee then began to brush her hair, staring at her reflection with a frown. Already her skin looked to have paled. She missed the sunshine. She missed the heat.

She missed…everything.

A knock sounded at the front door, and she moved to it slowly. When Elana stayed here, there was a security presence, but for Eloise, a lock was enough. She unclicked it and opened the door a crack. Then froze.

'Tariq.' His name burst from her lips, shock, confusion, anger, love and need tangling inside of her, filling her mouth with longing. He wore full Savisian dress, and he looked quite impossibly handsome. Her heart stammered.

'Eloise.' His eyes glittered when they met hers. 'Do you have a moment?'

As if she had anything else to do! But this was an impossible conversation. 'I thought I explained in my note,' she said quietly. Then, softer still, 'Did you get the note?'

'Yes, little one, I got the note. Now,' his voice was gruff, 'let me come in or I will bang this door down.'

She didn't doubt him, but even without the threat, she would have opened the door. It had taken all of her courage and strength to walk away from him once; she couldn't do it again, not just yet.

Strangely, her first thought was that she was self-conscious. She'd only worn long, flowing dresses around him before. And the caftan in the cabin. And of course, nothing at all on their last afternoon together. But this was different. Today, she wore western clothes, and somehow it felt as though it delineated an invisible line between them, emphasising how far apart they were, in reality.

Only Tariq wasn't looking at her clothes. As he swept into the entrance foyer, he only had eyes for her. Her face, her eyes, her lips, her hair. He stared at her until her heart almost burst from her body.

'Has it really only been five days?' he demanded, lifting his hands and cupping her face, holding her steady for his inspection, staring down at her until she was trembling.

'Tariq, stop,' she whispered, with barely any

strength, because being held by him, touched by him, was so, so good, so powerful, she could barely breathe. 'You can't be here.'

'Why not?'

'You know why not,' she responded quickly, the words breathy. 'You're going to marry my best friend. We can't do this. I won't.'

He moved his finger to her lips, pressing it there. 'How do you think I found you?' he asked gently, light reprobation in the words.

Fear twisted her heart. 'Oh, my God. You told her.'

'Yes,' he agreed.

She closed her eyes, stomach twisting. 'You had no right…'

'I had every right. Not only that, it was essential.'

She trembled for a different reason now, the betrayal eating away at her. 'Why?'

'Because she deserved to know.'

Eloise gasped. 'That's not your decision to make.'

His eyes narrowed. 'She deserved to know that we'd fallen in love,' he said quietly, and she sucked in an uneven breath, the admission that his heart was hers like a bolt of lightning. She basked in its light and warmth a moment before reality returned and she faced the original predicament head on.

'To what end?' she muttered. 'You're marrying her. Now you've just destroyed my friendship—'

'I am *not* marrying her, little one. How could I?'

She blinked up at him, her heart twisting. 'You *must*.'

'Why?'

'Because of your brother and your parents and because Ras Sarat *needs* you.'

'Ras Sarat needs an ally, and I will be that for them. But I can offer financial and trade support, and strategic regional assistance, without forcing Elana into a marriage she'd clearly prefer to avoid.'

Eloise's heart exploded. 'You'd do that?'

'Our countries have a history that goes back a long way. Of course I'd do that.'

'But what about you?' she asked, dropping a hand to his chest. 'You *need* a royal heir.'

'I need an heir,' he agreed. 'But the idea of making any other woman pregnant is anathema to me, so I think we should turn to a new plan. One in which you come back to Savisia as my fiancée. We'll arrange a quick wedding—after these past five days, I'd prefer not to wait at all, if I'm honest.'

Her head was spinning. It was all too much. She could barely keep up.

'But how could that possibly work? You're Spanish and I'm English. It's impossible to believe that I would ever be accepted by your people.'

'I am not Spanish,' he said with a shake of his head. 'I was born there, but my memories are of Savisia. I was reborn when my parents brought me home. Over time, I will work out how to marry the two distinct parts of me—the boy I was, and the man I've become. But either path leads me to the inescapable conclusion: I was raised to rule, just like you said. I enjoy the support of the people. If there is a civil uprising in response to my parentage, then we'll deal with that then, together.'

Her eyes swept shut. 'But marriage to Elana—'

'Cannot happen.' His nostrils flared, his eyes fired with determination. 'There are many things I would give up for my country, *habibi*, but a life with you is not one of them. Not you.' He dropped a hand, caught hers and lifted it to his lips, pressing a gentle kiss across each knuckle. 'I love you,' he said simply. 'And I need you in my life. Will you come home with me?'

She blinked up at him, her heart soaring, every part of her exploding. She tilted her head to the side, looking up at him for several beats, and she felt his worry, his doubt, and knew she had to put him out of his misery.

'I suppose I can risk one more flight, Tariq. For you, and the life we'll share together.'

'Actually,' he said, dropping his head and brushing their lips. 'I thought we could take the scenic route.' He kissed her slowly. 'What's the rush?'

They travelled across the channel by train, and then, once in Europe, Tariq drove them, through the vine-covered fields of France and the mountainous Alps, through ancient Croatian villages and into Greece, then they travelled in the Sheikh's magnificent yacht, across the Mediterranean until they landed at a port near the capital of Savisia. From there, things changed. She was no longer an advisor to the Crown Princess of Ras Sarat, but the fiancée of the Sheikh, and their relationship had to observe some more formalities. The yacht was met by a fleet of servants, fifteen of which were assigned to her, and several of which arrived with suitcases of clothes and jewels, so that when she stepped out into Savisia, she looked every inch the future Sheikha.

Her heart raced but then, she looked at Tariq and she knew there was no need to be nervous. Everything in her life felt as though it had been leading her to this point. Fate had always had this plan for her, she was sure of it.

Much to Eloise's delight, Elana was waiting at the palace, and Eloise cried when she saw her.

'You should have told me,' Elana chided gently, but hugged her best friend tight.

'I thought I'd ruined everything.'

'Instead, you made it a thousand times better,' Elana promised, reaching down and squeezing her hand. Eloise was then taken to the Sheikha, whom she had afternoon tea with, and after that, she met Graciano, Alicia and their children. By the end of the day, her head was spinning, and as happy as she was to be back in Savisia, she found herself longing for the sense of freedom their drawn-out trip through Europe had provided.

When she remarked as much to Tariq, he agreed. 'You know,' he said, leaning closer, 'I was thinking of taking a ride into the desert. I don't suppose you feel like joining me?'

She grinned up at him. 'I thought you'd never ask.'

The water still glowed with its beautiful phosphorescent algal bloom, but it was nothing to the brightness of their love and hope. Their future now secured, they had only to sit back and enjoy the ride.

Tariq had worried about how news of his parentage would affect the country, but in the end the focus was all on his marriage, his beautiful bride, and then, shortly afterwards, the announcement of her pregnancy. Far from any outcry over the lineage, there was universal adoration for the newest descendant of the royal family—and of course, that was how this child was viewed. The emphasis Tariq had placed on bloodline was, as it turned out, a far bigger deal to him than anyone else. Nonetheless, to avoid any future problems for his children, he had the Prime Minister introduce a referendum. The vote was overwhelmingly in favour of Tariq being acknowledged as the official and rightful heir to the Savisian throne. No challenge eventuated.

Years passed. Good, prosperous years for Savisia and, in time, Ras Sarat. Years of peace and fortune, years in which he felt grateful every day for the chance meeting with his wife, and the way they'd fallen in love.

They had four beautiful children, and when Annie, the oldest daughter of Alicia and Graciano, was finished with high school, their family relocated to Savisia, to be close to Tariq. Having missed so much of each other's lives, the brothers wanted to be as close as possible, and one of Tariq's favourite pastimes was hearing Graciano talk about their parents. His mother enjoyed this too, and had more or less become a de facto mother to Graciano and Alicia, whom she loved almost as much as she did Eloise.

Most importantly, Tariq came to understand over the years that family was about so much more than blood. Family was a choice one made, each day, to love and respect, to support and cherish, and with Graciano and Alicia, his mother, Elana and most of all, Eloise and their children, he felt the richness of his own beautiful, blended family.

He had been blessed, indeed.

* * * * *

If you were enchanted by
Desert King's Forbidden Temptation,
don't miss the first instalment in
The Long-Lost Cortéz Brothers duet
The Secret She Must Tell the Spaniard

And check out these other sizzling stories
by Clare Connelly!

Vows on the Virgin's Terms
Forbidden Nights in Barcelona
Cinderella in the Billionaire's Castle
Emergency Marriage to the Greek
Pregnant Princess in Manhattan

Available now!